Tales of the Unreal

Volume 2

Table of Contents

The Water Nymph

By PALMER ADAMS

SOMEWHERE, to some far and remote region, my father George Harper had gone. He had been missing since last Tuesday, and ever since I heard the news of his disappearance I, along with the rest of my siblings, have been restlessly searching for any clues that might bring us closer to explaining this shocking turn of events.

Out of all the leads and avenues of investigations we pursued, only one seemed to bear any fruit; he had been an artist all his life, and in his later years of retirement he had begun to paint prolifically, producing as many as two watercolor paintings a day. It was in his dusty attic, amongst the various stored paintings, that I found the first clue.

He had the habit of writing the dates for all his art, and it was while flipping through one of his journals full of pencil traced sketches that I realized the surprising and eerie trend which had overtaken his work. I had always known him to be primarily interested in landscapes and wildlife. The few of his

1

paintings that he had proudly displayed around his house were of looming mountains, fertile valleys and the like. Therefore it was an exceedingly strange thing for me to discover that, since November of last year, his paintings had consisted almost entirely of grotesque human figures.

I began examining these, and was greeted with men wearing indecipherable and alien masks, large processions holding ancient artefacts of unearthly origin and many other unsettling images; something about these scenes reminded me of the surreal and dreamlike paintings of the French artist Odilon Redon. Perhaps it was the blurred faces, or the ethereal color pallets used. Most likely, though, it was the inclusion of a single enigmatic creature that haunted the outskirts of almost all his paintings. Always was she depicted as floating in some body of water, a leering glare directed at the observer.

I examined this mysterious figure and saw her to be a woman with pale skin and dark hair. I stared at the various aquatic landscapes that she inhabited, the rolling seas and sunken cities, and as my eyes combed over her translucent body I felt a chill run up my spine. For despite her superficial beauty, her eyes were a deep and unearthly black that made me shiver. I wondered then what feverish visions must have overcome George in his old age for him to have developed this peculiar obsession.

Curious to see if any other information about George's mental state could be ascertained, I remembered that he had kept a diary too. After retrieving the brown book from one of his dusty cabinets, I skipped to the end and began to read. To my great dismay, it was almost entirely unreadable, consisting of schizophrenic and broken sonnets, odes to alien beings and long passages written entirely in unreadable foreign runes. Occasionally, there was a rushed illustration alongside these cryptic writings, often depicting that same water nymph that his later paintings had featured so prominently.

Right as I was about to put this cursed book away, I came upon what had to be one of the final entries in the book. After checking the date, I immediately recognized it to be in the week that George had gone missing. The entry was the same impenetrable scrawl as before, but between this manic writing I saw a faint glimpse of sanity; in big block letters he had written the address to a small town, a certain Arkhamsville. I consulted an encyclopedia and saw that the rural town was only a few miles away, positioned at the foot of one of the largest national parks in the country.

I felt a shudder of excitement at the reveal of this crucial clue. The page after it, too, had mention of this place, and it was there that I made out a hastily scrawled sentence, so unlike the noble runic symbols that stood alongside it: *In the lake my lover sleeps. She waits for me at river's end.*

I arrived early in the morning. My guides—two local youths who I had procured through a friend—were waiting for me, and greeted me with a wave. After conjoining with them and explaining my plan to follow the river upstream until I either found some hint towards George' fate or was forced to turn back, we set off from Arkhamsville and entered the wilderness.

For two days we travelled, my guides walking ahead and myself following behind. Sweeping mountain ranges characterized the sky and ancient oaks changed colors under a cool autumn sun. Along the way, I tried to engage my guides in conversation to gleam what information I could about the area. Frustratingly, they seemed entirely uninterested in talking, oftentimes simply ignoring me when I would ask them questions. Regardless, however, they did their jobs well and we made swift progress following the river through the dark forest.

I took great pleasure in the various flowers and creatures that we encountered along the way. Various species I had never seen before sprouted from sandy dirt along the riverside, and I enjoyed spotting those myriad types, remarking their exotic and wonderful forms. The journal I had brought along was put to good use, being the place where I sketched my impressions of the maroon birds and selenic willows I encountered. These feelings of curiosity, however, were only present during the day; the nights, in contrast, were significantly less pleasant.

The first night was disturbed and restless, my sleep being uncomfortable and short. For the rest of the day, my mood was worsened and I found I was needlessly irritable, getting upset at the slightest thing. The next night was even worse, for I awoke in a sweat, the result of some forgotten nightmare. Occasionally as I slept, I would hear a faint voice talking to me; the tone reminded me of my mother, and I concentrated as hard as I could to try and figure out what it was saying, but I was unable to do so. There was a faint desire I felt when I heard those incomprehensible words, which were often accompanied by an alien melody, and the thought of it disturbed me for I was not one to dream of such things. These dreams continued the further we progressed, growing more intense with each passing day.

Eventually, we arrived at a mossy bridge. I made to cross it, but was surprised to see both of my guides standing back. Their faces were anxious and they gestured with fear at the expanse of land the bridge led to. It was no different than the wilderness we had spent the past few days traversing, save for the fact that the river seemed to grow bluer and deeper on the other side of the bridge.

I approached them and asked what the matter was.

"We can't go there," one of them told me. "Nor should you, either. It is said that whoever passes over the bridge of Abalonia passes into the domain of ancient and magical creatures, the likes of which are hostile to mankind. It is not meant for any human visitor—there is a curse laid upon any traveler who dares cross, so that none who have crossed have ever returned."

I laughed, for these fears were of the vaguest, most superstitious and primitive quality. Seeing that they would not be swayed by any rational argumentation, I decided to continue without them. It was to my frustration that I had to embark on this next part of my journey without their aid, but I was determined to discover George's fate and so I pressed on.

They were correct that this land was different from the wilderness before it; for after I crossed the bridge, I noticed a subtle shift in the surrounding scenery. The plants grew older and stranger, sporting Paleozoic patterns and long forgotten colors. The oaks grew more twisted and closer together, oftentimes forming such impenetrable walls that I had to walk a long distance around them just to continue on my path.

I walked through these misty woods, making sure that I could see the flowing river at all times, and whilst I did so I contemplated my guide's warning. It was a source of humor to me, then, the suggestion that I had somehow stumbled or trespassed into a forsaken place. I wondered at what crude stories they must have told in that rural and perhaps backwards village that caused those young men to believe such things.

Despite these thoughts, however, my mind was not free of worry. As I journeyed through this evidently ancient and untouched land, an essence emanated from it that besieged the heart. A sense of awe awakened, true, but of awe touched somewhere by a sense of alarm. I noted the furtive whisperings of those huddled oaks and the complete absence of any human structure, lacking even the smallest sign of activity such as the remains of a fire. I felt I had travelled back in time to when the world was ruled by older and crueler things, and these feelings were coupled with the disturbing sensation of being watched that arose from the disturbing dreams I had of late; and all this woke in me the horrible possibility that perhaps the words of my guides held in them some semblance of reality.

As night fell, I set up camp nearby the river as I had done the previous nights. Again I heard that dreamlike melody calling me while I slept, but it was many times stronger now. It felt like whoever spoke these things was much closer; before they were muffled as one who speaks from a great distance, but they were now as clear as the speaker was leaning in next to me. As such, I could make out most of what was said. Please, the voice sang. I am so lonely. Come, visit me. These words stirred me with a great excitement, and all night I rolled around and moved in anticipation, listening to the melodies of my unknown interlocutor.

And so I dreamt of this voice, and it was in the early hours of the morning that I awoke, much before the sun began to dawn. My mind was still fatigued and dreary as I started to move around. With a tingling feeling on my neck, I realized that I could still hear the sounds of that ghostly voice even though I was no longer dreaming, and there was a dull urge inside that led me towards the direction of the sound.

I walked beside the shallow crystal river. In the horned moonlight I thought I saw malformed aquatic creatures riding on strange currents. The voice grew louder, the melody more haunting, and I finally came to a tangled wall of branches. Judging from the intensity of the voice, almost crying with desperation, I concluded its source must lie behind this barricade. I took a deep breath and burst through; branches cracked behind me and a group of birds retreated into the air, and then I was gazing at an open plateau.

The grass stretched forward before creeping downwards to a soft riverbank, which faded into a large circular lake. To the left of the lake there was a sandbank that separated it from the rest of the river I had so diligently followed. The tune was loud now, where it seemed to come from some antiphonal symphony, and the urge in my chest had grown to be unbearable, so that I could not help but approach this lake even further. I knew that whatever I was looking for lay in its depths.

I reached the edge and waded in; as I did so, there was a frightening change. Green though the water had been, it grew greener still. A thousand black tentacles writhed there like dark sea serpents. As I watched, too fascinated to be afraid, a pale disc slowly rose towards the surface. It was not until I had gone up to my waist that I was close enough to see what it was—and then only because it stared back at me. A face was looking through the water, half submerged, and I thought that it might have come from some alternative pseudo-planet, some antediluvian cousin of earth.

She must have been sixty feet tall at least. I felt her eyes crawl over me as she hovered in the center of that ancient lake. Her crimson lips broke into a smile, and I watched as it revealed an army of pointed white teeth; the tentacles I had taken to be sea serpents were strands of her floating hair. I realized, then, that this was the creature I was looking for, the same water nymph that had been George's obsession before he had disappeared.

"Do not be afraid," she said. "I have come for you." Her voice sounded like it was drawn from celestial flutes.

That frightful odalisque glided towards me. Beneath the silky surface, I could see the rest of her naked figure floating motionlessly; her long pale neck led down to translucent shoulders, and then the contour of her figure changed as two breasts hung from her delicate torso. If it were not for her grotesque and overwhelming size, she would have been the fairest maiden I had ever seen.

"You have heard me from far away," she said. "It is because I need you that I have called you here."

I stared at her. "Who are you," I asked.

"There is not time for trivial questions. This may be our only chance. Please, listen to me."

"You are breathtaking," I told her. "But I must know why I dreamt of you, and why others have dreamt of you too, and why men have gone missing when they pursue your strange calling."

She sighed, and her face fell into sadness. "See me. Know that I will not hurt you. That is my promise."

I asked her what she wanted.

"For you to come me into the waters with me, if only for a moment."

I must have been forty or fifty paces from her at least, for while she floated in the depths of the lake I clung near to the shore. Despite the powerful urge I felt to obey her, to plunge into her watery embrace, there was another part of me that hesitated.

"Am I not enough for you?" she called. "Where else have you seen such flawless skin? Such sculpted features? Why do you refuse me?"

I told her I didn't, only that I was nervous. I think this pleased her, for she let out a soft giggle upon hearing it.

"Hurry," she said, "we do not have long. Once the light touches these waters I will have to leave."

This time, when she spoke, she rose further out of the water. Now her whole head was above the surface and I was able to see her visage in full; small waves lapped around her neck from the ripples this movement had created. She truly was beautiful, in a way that was impossible to describe.

I watched as she extended one of her arms over the shimmering lake, so that her giant palm faced towards me, the tip of its fingers gently breaking the surface. Easily I could have reached it if I wanted to by treading towards where it waited for me. For ages it felt like I stood there, contemplating her offer; there was a deep stirring in my chest and my mind was intoxicated by the haunting melody that she sang, and I have never felt a longing so great in my life.

Finally, right as I was ready to step forward and join her, a chilling wind from the night air howled by, rousing me from this stupor. Suddenly I recalled the faint feeling of alarm that I had felt earlier, and realized it had grown into a full blown dread and panic! Something is wrong, I thought. Somehow, I had been too enthralled in her aura to notice it; but it became clear to me then and so I instinctively pulled back.

As I did so, the illusion snapped; no longer under her spell, I witnessed an infernal and hellish transformation. For while the water nymph had before appeared a young maiden, now she transformed into something monstrous and scarred. Her perfume, once so alluring, became a dark miasma that caused me to gag. Realizing that I had broken free of her enchantment, she leapt out of the lake towards me, exposing her full body. Without the support of the water her skin sagged and I saw the large patches of hair that clung to her bald scalp.

Beneath her, that once deep lake was now only a waist high pool. Its muddy bottom was littered with bodies, some of men and others unrecognizable, each at varying periods of decay; and out of all the terrible sights of that night, surely this was the most disturbing part, for in that rotten graveyard—and this I swear is true—I spotted the decomposing corpse of my father, George Harper.

I found myself crawling backwards up the riverbank, repulsed by this hideous thing. Meanwhile the water churned and bubbled, and I heard her let out a pained cry, so different from the melody she had sang for me that I wondered if I had not simply imagined the latter.

I ran away, crushing sleeping flowers with heedless feet and swearing never to return. Her voice called out to me, harsh and grating now, but this time I felt no desire. As I ran, my mind was maddened by the memory of that terrible sight that was her true form. And beneath the silver moonlight, those strange oaks and furtive animals glared at me and I felt like an unwelcome trespasser in that unfamiliar pagan place. So I did not cease my steps till I had retraced my entire week of travel in the course of a night, and it was outside their town, wandering madly and whispering meaningless things, that I was found by my two young guides.

It has been a month since then. With every passing day I regret my mistake more and more. What initial sympathy and sadness I held for George's demise has been sublimated into an envy for his fate, and every night I dream of her more clearly than I did even when I lay next to her ancient lake. I look back on my earlier reaction, my horror and revulsion, and I understand it no more than I understand the sayings of desert wanderers who speak in foreign tongues.

By now the urge has overtaken me. I can no longer work, or write, or even think about these things without that overwhelming feeling of sorrow and absence appearing in my heart; further, I know it can only be remedied through one means and one means alone. We cannot bear to be separated any longer.

This will be the last time you hear from me. Do not seek me, for I will not be found.

Quickly now, I must be going. She waits for me.

Vantablack

By Alex Beyman

HERE'S a few silver linings in all this. I think the original saying had something to do with clouds. That part's no longer applicable, of course.

For example, so much of my life until today was just one long, tedious struggle against entropy. Against the slow but steady breakdown of everything I worked so hard to build up, like painstakingly removing individual grains of sand from the bottom half of an hourglass and moving them back to the top.

That's all over now. I suppose poverty and hunger are as well. For that matter, today is the day that the shining dream of world peace has finally been achieved. I just wish there was somebody to celebrate with.

Instead I'm trapped in this blasted tin can, peering out the little window at a jet black sky, not a single star to be seen. A "hyperbaric chamber", I think. I'd only ever heard of these being used for diving before my doctor sent me to spend the night in one.

I can't say as I feel much better, though I doubt that's the chamber's fault. There's something about the certain knowledge that you're witnessing the extinction of humanity which ruins your appetite. That, and the realization that my last meal will be the meager tray of hospital food that the nurse slid to me through a little double doored airlock just before it happened.

All of a sudden, the sky turned black. Just like that. I was lucky enough to be looking out the window through the little porthole in the side of the chamber at the exact moment, though perhaps lucky isn't the word I want.

Didn't register at first. Thought maybe I was seeing it wrong. I still didn't understand what was happening as a distant airliner fell out of the sky. Nor when the couple walking by the waterfront a hundred feet or so from the hospital collapsed, clawing at their faces.

Birds also fell, one of them near enough to the window that I could see its eyes bug out, and most of the blood in its body boiling out its twitching, wide open beak. At the same time there was this violent wind... indoors.

I felt none of it inside the sealed chamber, pumped up to several times sea level air pressure, but I could see the effects making a mess of the hospital room. Papers swept about as if in a hurricane, which were stacked neatly on the counter a moment prior. The windows bulging outwards, then bursting in a shower of shimmering glass shards.

Then the glass of water the nurse forgot to send in with my meal began to boil away into the vacuum. I think that's when it dawned on me what'd occurred. Struggle as I might, I cannot clearly recall the nurse's face when she barged into the room.

I remember her hair, though. Whipped about, this way and that, like a television news reporter covering a record breaking windstorm. She kept pounding on the wall of the chamber as she collapsed against it. The metallic, resonating impacts continued for most of a minute... but grew progressively weaker until there was only silence. Perfect, everlasting silence possible only in the total absence of air.

She's still down there, slumped against the chamber. I feel certain of it. Mercifully, I can't see her through the porthole due to the narrow viewing angle. I don't know what I'm afraid of, it's not like she'll decompose. It's not like that collapsed couple outside, or anybody else, will ever decompose.

Kept perfect forever. Pristine, preserved, vacuum sealed. It still feels like a bad dream. Everything outside is still so colorful. Moreso than before if anything, without an atmosphere to scatter the light.

But oh, that contrast. That stark, absolute contrast. Of the green grass against the pitch black, starless sky...before the unfiltered sun started turning it brown. Or the trees, or the big colorful fiberglass ice cream cone atop the white truck at the far side of the lake, just barely visible from this vantage point.

The landscape looks like a paper cutout superimposed against the most intense, pure darkness conceivable. Gone is the soft, gentle gradient between sea level and space. Is there even still an ocean to measure that by? How long will that much water take to boil away? Hundreds of years? Thousands?

I don't begin to understand how any of this happened. That's what keeps me from fully accepting it. Every time I lay down to sleep, best I can in the cramped confines of this meager pocket of trapped air in an airless world, part of me expects to wake up to blue skies. Clouds. Birds singing, planes soaring overhead.

If there was a little television or something, maybe I could find out... but then, who could still be broadcasting? How many like me can possibly be out there, coincidentally sealed inside something airtight for whatever reason when humanity's final moment arrived?

Astronauts. Astronauts! There have to be some aboard the space station, right? How I wish I had a radio or something. At this point with so little life remaining, I would gladly trade some of those hours to hear another voice. Anybody's voice, lying to me... telling me this isn't the end. That somehow, things will be alright.

My phone, too. If there's still internet service, I might read the final thoughts of the last generation, immortalized. Frozen in silicon, even after the lights all go dark. Wind power is out, obviously. Hydro power is out. Solar still works. I assume nuclear still works.

It will all go dark soon enough, though. I just wish I knew why. It's the senselessness of how the human journey has come to an end that rips at my insides, as abruptly and violently as the sky was ripped away.

No holy book predicted this, that I know of. There nothing in the way of a warning. No alien invasion, no speech from the president, or commandments from the sky to build an ark. One moment the sky was there... then it just... wasn't.

I wish I could say it will all be figured out eventually, but there's nobody left to do that. Was I spared? Am I one of the lucky ones? Somehow I don't feel that way. ...Nuclear submarines! Those ought to be alright for awhile.

They make their oxygen from seawater, don't they? They'll starve long before they suffocate. I wish I knew how many were out there on patrol when it happened. For some reason knowing the exact number of remaining humans would be a comfort.

My stomach growls, reminding me that my own lifespan is also measured in food remaining on that tray. I nibble at the brownie, last one I'll ever taste. I'm painfully hungry. It's an alien sensation. I never knew what actual, desperate hunger was before this.

I always just ate the moment I felt the smallest pangs of hunger. Never giving any thought to how bad it can get. My mouth is unbearably dry as well, the moisture in the food my only source of water. I look longingly out the porthole at the glass on the cabinet, but of course it's bone dry.

I wonder if those astronauts will return to Earth. Where else can they go? Just to roam this abhorrent... vacuum Earth... in their space suits, until their oxygen runs out. I begin to wonder how long that would take. The printed labels inside this chamber say it has 72 hours of backup O2 and sodalime, for removing CO2.

I'm on day two now. I can't see the clock from this angle. I never realized before today how much I relied on the way the sky looks in order to get a feel for what time of day it is. Just before the nurse sealed me in this thing, I remember she mentioned something about a clown.

The sort that comes to cheer up terminally ill children. She mentioned something about a large order of balloons for him to hand out. Despite myself, I laughed as I imagined all of the balloons bursting at once when it happened, then falling limply to the floor all around his body like a bouquet of wilted flowers.

I scanned the city in the distance for any indications of fire from the plane crash, but of course there couldn't be. If by some miracle the cabin remained intact, everybody onboard would be in the same situation I am. Having the same grim thoughts about what to do with their dwindling time.

I suppose any planes that were taxiing on the tarmac at the airport would be fine... though what awaits the passengers in the coming hours would be worse by far than the comparatively merciful, rapid death of anybody caught outside.

I carefully savor the last of the peas and corn, which I'd originally planned to scoop into the trash when given this meal yesterday morning. What a difference a black sky makes to your perspective... to your priorities.

I then feel the ground shake beneath me. Gently at first, but the tremors grow stronger and stronger. Earthquakes? Too rhythmic, surely? It feels like something's getting closer. I cower within my little oasis until the tremors begin to weaken. Soon, everything is once again unnaturally silent and still.

There's another chamber across from mine. Empty, as luck would have it. I catch myself wishing there were somebody inside. Just someone to look at. To smile at, to cry with, though there's no way we could talk.

Anybody at all. My worst enemy. Just so I wouldn't have to face the end alone. More completely alone than I've ever been in my life. I fiddle with the emergency oxygen mask dangling from a hook on the chamber's inner wall.

That won't save me, will it? Anything I inhale into my lungs will only make them burst. It's not even the lack of oxygen that's the problem, but the lack of pressure. I know it's not like what happens in space movies, but that doesn't change anything. I wouldn't make it far.

There's a toilet, at least. I have no idea how it can flush without compromising the higher pressure in here. Just that when I flushed it for the first time after the sky turned black, the bowl did not refill with water. It just makes a gurgling sound.

I'm not yet desperate enough to drink out of there anyway, even if I could. As the sun slowly crawls overhead, it eventually reaches just the right spot that a beam of sunlight shines in through the porthole.

I withdraw from it the moment I feel the scalding heat on my arm. There's undoubtedly radiation to contend with as well, though in here I'm well shielded from it. Every possible option that occurs to me is stuck down just as quickly.

What's the point? What am I hoping will happen within the next 48 hours? Rescue? By whom? There's no reasoning with my instincts, though. However I wrestle with my primal urge to stay alive, I cannot subdue it.

I wish I could lay in the grass one last time and watch the clouds roll by. My body tenses up with anguish at the thought. Just one more time, feeling the soft blades of grass on my legs, neck and shoulders. Pointing out clouds which resemble dragons, ships, or whales.

In a fit, I twist the emergency pressure release. I hear a loud hiss, and feel an immediate change in my inner ear as the internal pressure begins dropping at the maximum safe rate. I pace back and forth, tugging at my hair, agonizing over whether this is really what I want to do.

I can't just hop back inside if I change my mind. There's enough gas to refill the chamber, but I'd be dead before it got back up to pressure. What else is there to do, though? What else is left? The sky is black. That's the hard truth of it. The sky is black, and I'm out of options.

Even when the pressure reads one atmosphere several hours later, I can't open the door. The differential between the inside and outside pins it shut. I scream at it, as if that will somehow loosen it up. I throw myself at it, shoulder first, over and over.

Each time the door budges slightly and I hear a brief, loud suction sound. Halfway between a burp and a hiss. Some air escapes during the split second when I run into the door! I redoubled my efforts, slamming into the door harder and harder until my shoulder throbs.

Doesn't matter. Nothing will ever matter again after this. Finally, the last impact budges the door enough that I can hold it open by about a centimeter. The rest of the air escapes in a powerful gust, tossing my hair like the nurse's.

My hospital gown at last stops fluttering once the last of the air finishes rushing out. Every inch of exposed skin hurts. I can see my veins bulging beneath my skin, and feel growing pressure behind my eyes. I close them and fumble around.

My hand brushes up against something soft. It's... hair? I open my increasingly bloated, bloodshot eyes. The nurse. Her skin is a mess, red and blistered from the sun. There are bloody spots all over her clothing wherever veins burst beneath it.

Not much time. I just want... I want to choose how it ends. I knelt, then lifted the stiff body of the nurse in my arms. I then stepped outside through the shattered remains of the window, indifferent to the sharp little bits sticking into the bare soles of my feet.

Twenty seconds? Fifteen? I knew it would be like this. But I only felt more and more certain that this is how I wanted it to happen. Once outside, I glanced around and noticed a van parked just in front of the hospital entrance which read "Salvador's party supplies". The driver was slumped over the steering wheel.

A man dressed up as a party clown laid in a pitiful, technicolor heap just inside the hospital entrance, surrounded by the shredded remains of burst balloons. Even now, I am still able to smile. Even now.

I can feel the strength draining from my sweaty, sunburnt

body as I trudge out onto the grassy expanse overlooking the lake. I remember watching the leaves of the nearby tree dancing in the wind on the day I arrived. Motionless, now.

I lay the nurse down in the grass, then ease myself down next to her. She might've been pretty before. Looks like it. Must've been a caring person too, if she went into nursing. How I'd have liked to say something poetic to her just now.

Instead I took her delicate, sunburnt hand in mine, and stared up at the empty black sky. A single tear escapes, then boils away into   the   vacuum.

Sleep of the Diviner

By Sophus

O H anoxia, that mindless dreamless sleep. To stagger along a road, fumes of what you were, to look down at a faded map melting in midnight rain without a clue as to what is happening. Heavy humid breaths all the way up another hill, empty air pooling in lung bottoms the whole way down. Asphalt slick with rain, sodden shoes fail to gain traction. Really, where was it that you were meant to be? The rippling haze of gray pines holds no answer, merely fencing in the road. The sun is long-set. It is getting cold.

There is hazy recollection near where the hill bottoms out. It was the mother's house up ahead. That was it. A vision of her, then, smiling in some warm kitchen, soft yellow light on her face, her crinkling eyes. Yes. She was up ahead. Where was it you were coming from? Harder to recall, head feels empty yet. Pestis swarm buzzing behind the eyes thick and slow, obscurant. You stand in the rain, straining against it. The hum subsides a moment and it comes back. Dropping off a package to your old friend, that was just earlier this evening. How long ago, when did your mind slip into the night and let you wander out here alone?

Glance at the map now, soggy and getting harder to read. Her home is four hundred miles off. No, wait. Four hundred? The peninsula is only sixteen across, it can't be… The mist has smeared it somehow, stretched the purple ink well, well beyond reason. Bands of it crawl along the page, wrapping around the dot where you should be. Blink and its gone, the words oscillating, yes, but inanimate. Another look, scrutinizing under the paltry street lamp. No, it was forty three miles, not four hundred. Of course of course! That, well… Forty three is still quite a ways.

With a start it becomes apparent that somehow you've moved quite a ways. Street lamps long gone, trees harrowingly dense on all sides in utter blackness. Bewildered, yet another glance at the map. Words stretch and bulge, ink taking new life, dancing around droplets and fingertips. Very odd, very strange indeed. Home is closer than initially thought. Those forty three miles were much further south, near the old galloping bridges, long past. There's a city rather close now but you haven't the slightest recollection of walking further than maybe five miles since delivering your package. Or walking while looking at the map for that matter. Have you?

The mother's face again, somewhere light and clean and seemingly forever away. But there are lights ahead already now. From the top of this last hill, the great pines wear thin enough to make out an overpass and the old paper plant. Quite relieving really. If nothing else it's possible to wait there till this spell passes and the head clears some. Maybe the rain will lighten too. Where is this again? Exit 18B$_B$. Ah yes, you know the one.

There are no cars. With sudden stupefying confusion you realize there are no cars anywhere on the road. This is a five lane exit onto a state highway and nothing. Silent. You start running. For no particular reason it becomes clear that there is someone behind you. Keep running until the exit goes up and onto the overpass and you are forced to slow. The overpass peters out and the trees recede fully into a murky skyline. The bike lane loops back onto an intersection far below, everything else just stops, rebar jutting into the empty air. You can feel him behind you right? Turn and nothing, left to survey the horizon in raging paranoia. The skyline is normal but dark, the familiar warehouses and short office buildings little more than a silhouette. Only the red warning lights twinkle and even then it is so soft you worry it might be something else entirely.

You step forward and hear a footstep directly behind you and taking another step you don't. His hand is on your shoulder. Spine grows black and necrotic with cold, T-5 frostbite as your ribs invert outward to jut like porcupine quills. Turning, it becomes obvious who this is. You don't recognize him.

Seen this before, haven't you? Nice night for a walk… Mmm that map is falling apart. How much further do you have to go?

His pallid skin shines like fishscale. Leaning forward his eyes bulge hideously, bulbous things too large for their sockets, aging whites almost wholly obliterated by pupil's black. Flabby, greasy, with a slick widow's peak to crown a stubby and misshapen body, it is a blessing his drab cloak conceals so much.

Don't let that map fall apart. Keep it together. Don't let it fade for your sake.

Empty smile.

You know you're going to die, right?

Spinal dread sprouts icicle wings. Trembling, oh god it's

Ha, I see it. You see it too. Try not to, please.

An overwhelming urge to vomit. Sudden stabbing hunger. The man sticks his left hand out as if to shake. It is gloved in red leather. Puke burns the back of your gums. He delicately pulls the glove off and tosses it from the overpass. His hands are ruined. Mess of scarring and gnarls, something like grubs where fingers should be. Marble skin mottled in jaundice yellow.

You have the strongest urge to bite off his fingers. You grab his hand and stare him in the eyes. His mouth grows larger and larger as he screams in glee, eyes widening to absurd proportions. Shaking, his hand pushes closer to your mouth. You throw it down, collapsing. He hollers something incomprehensible. It feels like the asphalt is digesting you. He looks down at your shaking frame.

Leave, leave leave. Leave. Ha, but they'll leave without you. That map is melting. You won't make it. Cross the bridge, but not make it. They'll have you too they will.

He turns then and walks off, rapidly fading into the dark. There is traffic noise. Standing, there is light in the city. The overpass is not connected to the exit, but to the intersection as it should be. There is no bikeline and the road does not stop in space anymore. Strangely, this is relieving. You hurry down this new stretch to the sidewalk below.

The intersection is much quieter, the cars absent again. There are two parking lots diagonal from each other, empty save for one overturned wheelchair. On the right is an abandoned casino guarded by cracked totems, their lifeless eyes, amphibian and corvid, rotting in some perverse new sky-burial. The building itself is partially collapsed and rain streams from crooked marquees onto the revolving doors.

Faint light hums up ahead on the left, an old drug store apparently still open this late. Shelter. There might be others there. Fear. But it passes and as the building grows closer whatever reservations one might have vanish. For a moment it is like living normally again. Walk to a friend's place to give a gift and converse, stop somewhere for snacks, come home late at night to a worried mom...

But there is no one in the building, and the lights are much too dim. Every shelf in the row stands empty, vertebrae of a picked-clean carcass jutting from the dirty linoleum floor. Behind the cash register there is a faint mewing, nearly inaudible. It grows panicked as you approach, thumping and shrill yelps increasing in frequency. Hesitate right in front of the register, steeling yourself for a glance.

It is a newly hatched bird of some sort. Naked, infant thing stretched to nearly human proportions. Eyes sealed and beak hanging weakly open, far too large for the head which lulls against the counter. Ants the size of soda cans are dragging pieces of its flesh away one after the other, gnawing at its scaly legs and broken wings. Its disassembly is immaculate, done with timepiece precision, total efficiency. The bird appears to be weeping. The ants have started on its liver. Transfixed you watch the line continue on, ant to ant to ant in a great chain that carries this creature's being somewhere else, to be something else. There is a fuzzy sort of feeling that this has happened before. In the ants you see his dull visage and know that he is standing beside you in this scene and there is nothing to be done. You see them start to go for its eyes.

You turn to leave the store and go only a few paces before spotting an ant on the ceiling, which crawls along until one of the molding panels gives out and it falls upward into the gap. The panels begin to fall and shatter sporadically. You gaze at the space behind them and feel leaden. There is an immense piece of stone there, panels falling away to reveal sanskrit and cuneiform, ancient carvings of El and thundering bulls, the start of columns and reliefs of the old kings. The Tree of Life looms down, the fallen ant prostrating across Keter. Throaty shrieks begin.

I was once Thoth! I was once fed on their tripe!

Was that the bird or you? Shrieks grow louder and mean nothing. Damned and dying. Floods of guilt come down.

All at once a great hand pulls away the ceiling, the stonework, the sky itself. Above glows the three and also a bitter fourth, the crown, its others, and the usurper, seed of the bull and heart of the heavens. Some great tear in nature itself. The distinct feeling of pressure in the skull, eyes rolling out of their head maybe. He is there too, he is there and the hand, ghostly and featureless, reaches down and opens the till of the register, collecting its meager contents.

It drops two drachma at your feet and leaves.

Everything returns to as it was. You lie there weakly. The ant falls onto your legs. You shake it off and stand, unsure. The bird is fully quiet now, ants uninterrupted in their grim march. You need to leave.

Halfway out the door there is a sudden voice from behind the counter, soft and sweet—

Sir, is something the matter?

A young woman is standing there, little red vest muted by cold fluorescence. Her gaze meets your own through a now-spotless convenience store, ceiling intact and shelves stocked. Looking at her things now appear as they should be and all animal anxiety melts away.

Sir, can I help you with anything?

You are at the counter, looking at her. Hazel eyes behind wisps of blond hair, messy ponytail over a shoulder. Her nose is like your mother's, but familiar in some other unplaceable way. She stares with tender affection. Her arm reaches out as she leans across the counter, hand reaching to cup your face. You bow into her kiss and run fingers through the loose hair draped along her ears. Hands run over flesh, teasing under shirts and into pant buttons. She slides a thumb into your mouth as the kiss breaks. Pulling away you can see that her eyes are empty. She wears an idiot smile.

With a slow pull she slides the map onto the counter. With lurching dread you watch a single large feather tumble to the floor as her vest slips. Her pupils dilate wildly and she begins tearing at the map, clumps of wet paper shredding to nothing. You feel the urge to eat her hands, teeth grinding into the flesh of her thumb. She begins gibbering. You grab the map as she attempts to pry her hand further inside you. Skin pressed to the point of breaking. She begins to shriek as you push her away and run from the store, teeth aching in want.

Footfalls echo behind you, broken only by her howling. It feels like half an hour before it can be certain she is too far behind to follow. You pant and clutch your side, looking about. The city stretches in odd dimensions and it is not clear where you are or how you got there, the mad chase leading to unknown places. Whatever landmarks there were, though inconsistent in their shape, now lay lost behind the droning haze. It is blacker yet, a night that will not break. It begins to pour.

The map is nearly worthless now. Erratic gaps and yet further sogginess have made things nearly impossible to discern. The industrial zone, your only guess at what the surrounding area is, stands four miles south of the highway out of the city. There should be an on ramp that eventually leads there but nothing nearby indicates where it is in proximity to you. Every road seems to loop back on itself, odd contortions of what should be city blocks. Your lungs burn yet.

You attempt to fold the map but it crumples and melts away in your hands, blue ink running along palm lines, stretching them into new shapes, the last pulpy scraps of industrial boundaries bleeding into your very life as it disintegrates completely. There is nothing left and a great hollowness descends, stained hands trembling.

Each of the four roads in front of you have obvious outcomes. Though obscured by fog the man's words repeat and despair takes over. It will all loop back.

You choose the third from the leftmost path and the city recedes rapidly, road once again enclosed by towering pines, sky darker than when you started. The trees loom over, bent as though thankful for your return. The road seems without end. Something running behind you, a man and a woman. The woman from the store, but how?

Run and run fast. Run imagining the route home from fragments of map and memory. Down hills and up until legs seize in pain. Up ahead are bridges, an escape, if only you can make it. Or weren't those the bridges from much earlier? Great suspension bridges, green with age and leading into pitch darkness. With sudden insight it becomes obvious that you'll never make it.

The two catch up to you, flanking either side, running with vigor incomprehensible. They smile as they run, unblemished joy, empty impossible grins beneath dead and blackening eyes. They yell in unison

Have me! Have me! Have me! Have me!

The man grabs your arms and wrestles you still as the girl forces her hands into your face. The urge flares as your lips part, her nails scraping past your front teeth. Some immense heat rises in your chest and you bite down.

You're too late! You're too late!

Blood pools in your mouth as they scream and howl, a jackal's ragged laughter. The loose flesh of her fingers rolls along your tongue, bone starting to splinter against molars. Swallow and blindly bite again. Sink into cartilage. You stare dimly at the fading bridge, so close to you, as it loses meaning. Seen it before but still it happens. The woman moans in ecstasy and his clammy fingers close around your throat. The bridge rushes towards you but it never quite meets, the rush of an infinite gap before blackness.

Before They Fall

By V. Bellingham

BEFORE they fall. Don't know when they'll be here. It's on every TV, radio station, and website. It's coming. Everything is telling me it's coming to a close. Sounds of weeping outside. People with paper white skin haunt the streets like phantoms. Smoke grows from the center of the city like a great, gray weed. I'll go to the liquor store. It's the end and there's nothing we can do. I need a drink. Something to smoke. Six months of sobriety for nothing. Out of the house and past the park. I used to take Madeline here. She's with mother. About a hundred miles away. Never see mother again. Father died two years ago. Never see him again. Madeline. Let it be quick. I hope the searing pain lasts a brief second. Where do you think we'll go? Blackness. Nothingness. I'm having a hard time imagining it. Crumpled emergency vehicles, dead first responders hanging out of broken glass. Porky Pig style. That's all folks. Bloodied heathens ransacking every store on main street. Abandoned vehicles litter the street. A man is naked like a shaman on top of the pharmacy roof. Meditating. Praying. Last man leaves the liquor store. Last man enters the liquor store. Pools of beer, wine, whiskey, broken glass. Looks like puddles of blood and urine. It could be blood and urine. Find a bottle of whiskey. Grab it. Take a drink. Burning sensation feels good. Hot coal down the esophagus and into the stomach. I'm dizzy. Jets fly overhead, deafening sonic screeching. Where are they going? They won't save us. No one can save us. Annihilation is imminent. I think if there is more I could have done. More I could have been. It really doesn't matter. Up to this moment it seemed like everything mattered. That it was all building up to something. But it's meant nothing. Claire is somewhere with her new husband. They'll probably die in each others arms. My life was in shambles before this, but I still had hopes, dreams. I could have turned it around. Not anymore. People are hanging from the street lights. A man with a gaping wound in his head sits on his lawn, mechanically picking grass, blank-faced. Next to him a woman's brains hang out of her head. She's gone limp. It'll be here before she even goes cold. The anticipation is getting too much to bear. I could hang myself. No. I don't have the courage for it. Whose fault is this? I don't know, and at this point in the chaos, I don't think it matters to a single soul. I will die with this bottle of whiskey. Thinking about driving the car as fast as I can. As far as I can. To see Maddy. No one can stop me from drinking and driving now. Can't out run what is coming. I'll never make it. The sound of sirens is dying out. Emergency services will soon give up. Half the bottle is already gone and I'm not even back home yet. Maybe I should join my neighbors. Gun shots, tires screeching, metal creaking and groaning. I imagine some will be safe. The rich are already in New Zealand by now. They've probably known what we just found out for at least a week. They were acting fishy. Looking back now it seems rather obvious something bad was going to happen. President giving heartfelt messages to the American people. CEOs resigning left and right. Stock market tanking. Now that it's here it doesn't feel real. I guess they'll rebuild over our ashen corpses. It's coming, but when? Maybe it's all theater, and we'll all be safe at the end when this all blows over. Perhaps it's a nightmare. Or a pleasant dream. A figure in black coming across the sky to blot out the sun. His robe opening, revealing death. Everything is technicolor. The sky angelic and open. I wish I could jump into it like a pool. Race, political affiliation, religion. None of it matters now. Newscasters say their goodbyes. Their eyes swollen with tears. If it comes and nobody's alive to remember it, did it ever happen? My problem flies through the sky like a Valkyrie. Revelations. The Antichrist. Beasts in the sky. Madeline. Mother. Claire. Old dogs I've had; Byron, Fluffy, Peanut Butter. The office. Bleach walls. Cork board notices. Simon handing out coffees. Everyday like that. At home. At the office. At home. At the office. Spent half my life before glowing screens cutting through darkness. Useless activities. Hobbies I've enjoyed all my life. Useless. I'll be none of them. Wherever I go I wonder if I'll see them there. I wonder if there's fishing and television and peace and never raining. Cloud bed in the heavens. Never need to fluff a pillow or toss and turn. If there is a hell I hope I won't be there. This already feels like an eternity of suffering. It's only been twenty minutes. Don't know if I could do another eternity. God, Vishnu, Krishna, Jesus, Buddha, Allah, Satan, anyone. Please help. Swat the flies from the sky. Cast them into the sun. A burning furnace. There is screaming and hysteria and chaos. They're closer. It's a blink of an eye. People murdering others just to feel something. Men and women running in the streets naked, genitals cooling in the summer breeze. There is laughter too. Some people are relieved, overjoyed. Why haven't we been raptured? Is there a god? Why would he let this happen? No it's us who have caused it to happen and it was only us who could have stopped it. People are masturbating in the open and holding orgies. There are orgasms happening in public. Blood covered and semen stained and horrible and beastly. It's all the last time. Last time I'll blink, think, drink, breathe, swallow, rub eyes, touch genitals. Here it comes. It grows louder. Screaming in the sky. Death is around me. He's calling me. His skeleton hand reaches out to me. People are still

29

evacuating. There's nowhere for them to go. It's just to comfort them. We used to have drills for this. Light, dark, sun, moon, sky, earth, asphalt. Had three car crashes in my entire life. Remember when I flipped in the jeep. Four houses I've lived in. Two women I've had sex with. One daughter I love. Never see her again. I think I see it. A brilliant flash. Waves blowing wood, stone, flesh, and bone apart. Deafening silence. I can hear my heart beat, my stomach digest, my lungs filtering my lasts gasps of oxygen. It's a skyscraper of a cloud. Broken glass. Squealing. I'm hungry. I'm scared. I'm drunk. My hands tremble. This is the last time I'll ever be. Let me take another drink. I missed this. And even if…

Muriel's Intruder

By K. R. Hartley

LOW clouds reared over the country and spilled like pitch onto the prairie, slow and wet and green at the edges. They wafted hither, the black fires approaching, and reigned across the gloam in small flickering sheets of light, fireflies like dragons in the reach. The sky blinked and faded and fell to the wind and the rinse came through in sharp sweeping parries that bent the horizon homeward and called the air into long bands of water.

An engine emerged from the damp, headlights growing in the fog. The pickup truck jumped and sputtered over the gravel and spat up mud and growled into the wash. The driver mumbled and swore to himself.

Inside a livingroom a young couple laid across a fur before a lit hearth, beaming into one another, eyes locked. They spoke with their hands and shared in their love while the weather spread the rooftop with a ceaseless patter and ran down the windowglass. Light filled the scene and cast shadows of bodies in rhythmic embrace, the thunder tumbling aloud and rolling in from the corners. Their voices piqued and wavered, sweat on their shoulders as they moved to the push and the pull, smiles to frowns to smiles again. They held up and steadied themselves against the wood, rocking into eachother, connected at the hips. Fire and lightning coursed through the room and somebody whispered and the lovers gave way and slumped across the rug. The young man gestured and the young woman reached behind them. She produced a cigarette and lit it and spoke.

"I want to paint the ceiling."

He looked up. His chest lifted and dropped with his breath. "You want to paint the ceiling?"

"I'm always staring at this ceiling. I want to paint it."

He closed his eyes and smiled. "What color?"

"Maybe a deep red. Like a menstrual red. Or a dark quiche."

He opened his eyes and blinked. "—A dark quiche."

"Yes. A dark quiche. Like a mustardy khaki. A burnt, mustardy khaki."

He cleared his throat. "Or—a deep red."

"Menstrual."

He repeated her.

"Adam. I want to have your baby."

He shifted himself and took her in the eyes and nodded his head. "I know."

She pulled herself up onto him and offered him the cigarette and he took it from her fingers and brought it to his lips and drew on it.

"First the ceiling." He tilted his head and pushed smoke into the room.

"I'll get pregnant if you come inside me all month."

He closed his eyes and nodded his head. She took back the cigarette.

"I already have a name." She rolled to his side and settled herself.

He lifted his finger and quieted her.

She pushed his hand away. "I want to tell you the name."

A sudden knocking startled the room and they both turned toward the door.

"Adam?"

"Hold on." The knocking sounded again and he stood and dressed himself and approached the noise. The woman covered herself in a quilt and knelt.

He pulled at the door and opened it to the storm, a rainsoaked man, troubled eyes darting. Adam spoke.

"Are you okay?"

"I need to use your phone." The man ducked in the rain and peeked into the home. "It's an emergency."

"What's happened?"

"Just need the phone. That's it."

"What's the emergency?"

"Crashed my car."

"Where?"

"Crashed my car and I need to use your—"

"Where did you crash your car?" Adam leaned forward. A pickup truck rumbled by the gate. He stood back.

"That's my friend's truck. I borrowed it to get help. I need to use the phone so I can call an ambulance. Because my friend is hurt."

"Your friend is hurt?"

"Please let me—"

"I can call the cops for you. But you can't come into this house. There is no—"

"No! Don't call the cops. No. I need to call my girlfriend. To come get me. And—" The man turned and glanced at the truck before he came back. "And take me to the crash."

"Where did you crash the car?" Adam shook his head and the man leaned in and glimpsed the livingroom.

The young woman caught the man in the eyes and shouted, a shrill gasp. She screamed at him. "No! Fucking god!"

Adam turned to her and gestured. "Honey?" He came back to the man. "I'm sorry but—"

The stranger leaned into Adam and put his foot on the sill and

Adam put his palm against the man and pushed him back out and shouted something. The man threw his arms up.

"Let me in your—I need to use your phone!"

"Get the hell out of here!" Adam waved his hand and the man flinched and slipped to his knee and stood.

"Please!"

"Go! Now. Or I'll call the police."

The man glared at him and shook his head and swore. He turned and returned to the truck and went inside and drove away. Adam followed with his eyes as it left. He came back and closed the door.

She dressed herself and came to him. "Oh my god." Her eyes were wide as she repeated herself.

"Are you okay?" Adam led them back to the hearth.

"Did you see him? His—face?"

"I saw him, Honey. I was right there."

"What was wrong with his face? Oh my god!"

"What?"

She closed her eyes and put her head down. "That was—so awful." She lifted her head and shuddered and they sat on the fur. "Babe. That was so awful."

"What?"

"Oh my god. You saved us. He was going to kill us. Adam! He was going to kill us."

"What?"

"Adam. Which way did he go?"

He tilted his head and pointed. "East."

"Adam. You need to call Muriel."

"Call Muriel?"

"He tried to come in here. Inside our house. Adam, what the fuck?"

He stood and went toward the table and addressed the telephone and put it to his ear.

"Adam. Did you see his—"

He put his finger to his lips before he spoke. "Hi Muriel. It's Adam. From next door. That's right. Hey listen, Muriel—"

The old woman sat in her rocker, the television glow dashing the room and twisting on the walls. She leaned forward and reached for her remote control and turned off the television and painstakingly stood herself up. She turned on a nearby lamp. "He what?" She came across the room to her frontdoor, the telephone cable coiling and stretching as she moved. She touched the knob and secured the lock. "Say that again?" Muriel pressed a switch and the porchlight shone through the etched pane. She put her head to the peephole and came back and turned and stepped to the middle of the room, listening. "Okay. Okay, thank you. Yes I will. Thank you." A tomcat circled her feet.

An enormous pounding boomed on the door and Muriel dropped the handset and let out a noise. The cat scattered. She bent and picked up the telephone and walked it back and hung it up and turned to face the door, light distorting at the glass. The pounding came again and she hesitated before stepping forward and leaning into the peephole. She studied for a moment and cried out. She came back and bent in a panic and touched the floor. Her voice shook as she swore and stood and turned out the porchlight and moved through the room, her body limping and her arms guiding her way.

She left and turned on a light and came to the end of a hallway, choosing a door and pulling it open. She dug through her effects and mumbled, coaching herself aloud. Out from the closet her belongings banged to the floor and mounted, boxes, tools, a vacuum cleaner. She stepped back into the mess, rattling her balance, a shotgun in hand. Over the pile she clamored and came to her knees and sideeyed the chamber before flipping it and checking the receiver. She stood and returned to the closet, rummaging and cursing. The pounding came once again from the frontdoor and Muriel whimpered and condemned herself. "Where? Where?"

She fell back again, over the heap and into the hallway, still clutching the gun, her free hand against the wall. She left into the frontroom and around a corner and addressed a door and opened it cautiously.

In the garage the orange bulb buzzed and the rain tapped the roof. She went down some steps, her hand on the railing, eyes on the floor. Behind her the cat came through a small specialized opening near the bottom of the door and made a noise. She edged around her sedan. The garage entrance had almost a foot of clearance. The rain smacked the concrete outside. She found herself across the room and began poking through storage, bins stacked against the wall, small cubbies of smaller boxes. Over her shoulder she looked to the entrance and returned. She pulled open a box and bent to her knees and loaded the weapon, pushing in the shells before flicking the barlock and standing. She braced herself and racked the bar and checked the safety and moved. On the ground the damp touched her slippered feet as she came around the sedan, up the steps and back into the house. She locked the door behind her.

Muriel crept into the frontroom shouldering the weapon and stepping in aim. Her shadow filled the space as she moved past her rocker and bent and turned out the lamp and addressed her telephone. She let the barrel to the floor. She put the telephone to her ear and dialed and waited. The pounding came again, this time extended, a long and angry hammer.

"Yes! Police!" The line clicked and she spun to face the door.

In a dimlit office a young woman tapped on a computer and touched her ear, her headset emitting a beep and her monitor glowing alight. "Nine one one. Police emergency. What is your address?"

"Seventeen twelve east township rangeroad. Saratoga. By the state trailhead."

"One seven one two east township rangeroad in Saratoga county? You said it's by the park entrance?"

"Yes! Please hurry! Somebody is at my door and they are aggressively knocking and my neighbor called and—" She turned and looked past the corner, through the kitchen. "My backdoor!" She dropped the handset and rushed herself out of the room and into the kitchen, shotgun in hand. She locked the door and turned back and came to the telephone and bent and addressed it again. "I'm sorry! I had to lock my backdoor!"

"Ma'am. Are you calling from your house?"

"Yes!"

"Is this a cell phone you're calling from?"

"No! This is my—my telephone!"

"Okay. A landline. Is it a cordless phone?"

"No!"

"What is your name?"

"But the cord is very long. I'm an old lady. I'm eightyone years old!"

"Ma'am—"

"Muriel Marie Bennett!"

"Okay. Muriel. I'm going to get you to stay on the phone with me. Okay?"

"Okay."

The sound of glass broke like an explosion from the kitchen and Muriel screamed and dropped the handset. She spun and shouldered the shotgun and disengaged the safety. The backdoor was clear. Slowly she sidled, her legs crossing under her nightgown, her head turning. She came to the staircase.

"The police are coming!" She stepped up onto the stairs, her frail legs inching, both hands on the weapon. With her back against the wall she settled herself down onto a step and brought the gun to her waist and pushed the stock behind her. "The police are coming right now!"

"I just need to use your phone!" The voice came from beyond the corner.

Muriel sobbed aloud before she reined herself in and shouted. "No! You have to go! Please! I have a gun!"

The man moved, unseen in the kitchen, swearing to himself. He called out something obscene and Muriel steadied herself. He came into view and once again she saw his ghostly visage, violent and desperate, a nightmare in his eyes. She opened the weapon with a mighty blast and the walls broke apart and the wood splintered and fell to the floor. Her breath hovered. The banister before her had blown away and the corner to the kitchen was marked in tatters. She screamed and racked the bar.

The man swore and showed himself again, a kitchen knife in his grip. Muriel sprayed, this time spinning him to the carpet. He immediately faltered to his feet and came at her, lunging and falling onward. She racked the bar as he came upon her and she cried as he wrestled her down the stairs to the landing. She kicked and wailed and crawled to her knees and fell. The intruder thrust the blade with his full weight and plunged her and pulled back and thrust again, missing. She moaned and crawled up on her back and collapsed.

The man stood and stepped over her and went to the telephone and hung it up. He searched the lamp with his hand and turned it on and picked up the handset again and dialed. After a moment he spoke.

Muriel ached aloud and grunted as she scanned her body with her hands and touched her wound. She looked at the man over her shoulder. He was now shouting into the telephone. She came back and found the shotgun, bottom of the stairs. She swung herself over and crawled to the landing, rolling herself and holding her breath. She came onto it and searched the floor and found it and took it up and spun and knelt. She brought it in aim and opened it, her body thrown back to the wood by the weapon. The man flailed and swore and ran to the frontdoor, fumbling for the lock. Muriel pumped the bar and aimed. He pulled on the door and made his exit and the door swung and gave way to the wind. She fired again. The door split apart and slammed itself closed and Muriel put the gun down and came to her feet. She bent for the weapon and stood and brought up another round.

She moved through the frontroom and instinctively replaced the telephone onto its hook as she passed. It rang immediately and she stared in a fix before she turned away and made herself out of the room, around a corner and into the garage.

She snuck down the steps and sidled to the door of her sedan and pulled it open and ducked inside. The shotgun came across her lap. She reached up and touched a button and the garage entrance jerked and opened itself to the storm. The wind shuffled the trees and the long bands of rain tilted and broke onto the ground. She started the car and pulled it into gear and drove.

Through the wash she careened the vehicle across the slick of the mud and into the man's truck. Her driverside window came to pieces and she leaned out. The driveway was blocked. She pulled the sedan into reverse and cut around on the grass to face the house. She moved the shifter and edged the car forward.

From the murk the man came upon the hood, his arms over him and his mouth wagging. He was speaking but she could not hear him. She put her foot to the floor and the man came across the windshield and in a moment she had dozed them through a wall and into a bathroom, glass and mortar and metal. The man struggled and whined, pinned in the wreckage. Muriel opened the door and came outside, pulling the weapon into both hands and struggling over the lawn. The man rolled over his shoulder and broke free.

"My cat!" She screamed and staggered into the night and the man crawled away. As she walked she turned and opened the weapon in his direction and was thrown to the dirt. She stood and pumped it and continued. She came around the side of the house to the backyard and found a hatch and pulled on it and went down into the cellar.

Through the dark she found her way with her hands and led herself past the roots and the wines and the preserves, up to a small flight of stones. She mounted them and came to the top and opened the door and stepped into the house with the shotgun in front of her. From another room she could hear the man's voice, a conversation. She stepped in silence and rounded a corner and came to the landing. In the frontroom the telephone cord stretched out of sight. Muriel spun and cocked her head to listen but could discern no words, an angry voice, fearful and dire. She backed herself up the stairs, step for step, the weapon looming. Quickly she turned and hurried upward and chose a door and locked herself inside. Atop the bed the cat called to her and curled into itself.

Her feet shuffled across the floor, careful and quiet. She

addressed the bedside table, the telephone. She gently lifted the handset and put it to her ear.

"Wait. What was that? *What was what?* That click. Hold on."

She swore and put the telephone back on the hook and made herself around the bed to the bedroom closet. She pulled it open and climbed in and sat and pushed herself to the back, the stock of the shotgun against the wall behind her. She stretched herself and closed the closet door with her leg. A voice came out and the bedroom door pounded and shook. She leaned forward and squinted through the thin horizontal slats.

The noise broke her nerve at every blow. The man was now kicking the bedroom door in, the lock bouncing and settling back into the jamb. He shoved ahead and his leg split the wood and the man put forward his weight and crawled into the bedroom through the broken door. He stood. Through the tiny space she eyed him. He knelt and looked under the bed and stood and said something. He faced the closet and stepped toward her. Muriel leaned back and breathed and squeezed the trigger.

The closet door blew out like matchsticks and the man reeled backward onto the bed and cried like a dog. Muriel stood and picked up the weapon and shouldered it and stepped out of the closet. She pumped the gun and pointed it at the man. He writhed on the bed next to the cat, quiet but for some muted squeaks. She sidled toward the window and looked out, still in aim, she came back. The man rolled himself and fell to the floor. He lurched toward the door, bloodied and coughing. Muriel leaned and pushed the window open and looked out again. The wind howled through the trees and sent their branches trembling and grasping at the air. She looked back to the man. He grunted to his knees, one foot up, and another, and stood. The tomcat came up and jumped from the bed to the floor, up over the sill and outside of the window. The telephone rang. Muriel dropped the weapon and lifted her leg and swung herself through and ducked out onto the roof.

In a moment the glass shattered behind her and the man fell into her, the pair of them rolling and bouncing on the tin roof.

They floated away and went against the dirt, landing in a pile, twitching and crying. Muriel was spread atop the man, wincing and holding herself. She budged and came over him and rolled off, staring up. In the sky the clouds moved like ribbons and pulsed with light. The weather fissured and the water rinsed her face and her nightgown blew to her waist. She mustered herself to her knees, hands to her mouth, and vomited, the foam spilling through her fingers. She let go and touched the grass. She stood and wavered and steadied.

Over the lawn she limped and dragged herself to the gate. Cinching by the truck, she walked out to the highway, clay on her legs and blood on her gown. The water came over her and the thunder banged on into her head and out through her feet and into the ground. Down the mud road she struggled and fell and stood again and continued. As she trudged the growl of a vehicle sounded from behind. Muriel dropped to her knees and put her hands in the muck and closed her eyes.

Past her the pickup truck sped and spat up water. Her body collapsed, submitting to fatigue, laying itself down and recoiling. She watched ahead. The truck swayed and jerked and skipped awry, wobbling to the shoulder before smashing hard into a large elm, an enormous bang. The hood drew up in flames which jumped to the cabin and dripped to the road. After a moment a fireball took its place and Muriel wept and rolled to her back. The blaze cracked against the rain and the smoke sank away. There she prayed and waited as the clouds brought her to a soak and the thunder roared over her cries. Through her tears the lights twinkled and spread themselves, blue and red, the sirens wailing. She clutched her wound. From behind her came a familiar noise and she turned, the tomcat, drenched and bleating aloud.

And in the livingroom the lovers' shapes broke and flashed against the wall, the light whipping with the hearth and dancing in from the window. They moved in unison, a raging and cyclical force, wild prosody on their tongues, sweat cast to the floor. Someone whispered something and they came to their backs.

"Adam."

He made a noise.

"Do you think she's okay? I hope she's okay."

He adjusted himself and crawled on top of her. "I want to have your baby." His eyes burned in the fervor.

"I was thinking."

He nodded and looked over his shoulder and came back. "I know. A dark quiche."

"We'll name him Adam. If it's a boy."

"And if it's a girl?"

She smiled and inched herself downward, filling her body and closing her eyes.

Colder Than Ice

By L.A. Labuschagne

THE last gas station on a midnight road to Hell, and Revere had the luck to find it before her pursuers. She reached its convenience store a moment later with relief bright in her eyes, and an arrow buried in her shoulder. Slung over the other was a satchel stuffed to bursting with canned food that, technically, belonged to them, the spiky types chasing her. And slung over the convenience store's doors was a padlock that had been rusty for decades.

Revere's knees would've gone weak if not for the adrenalin and the cold. Instead, she stiffened, and swung her gaze. First left—the pumps and their solitary slashed-tire car, and behind them a dilapidated car wash with its roof fallen in and its equipment dragged out front and broken apart. All of that under a starless, ever-present sky. Looking bleak as the bloodthirsty shouts of her three victims grew ever louder.

A look right was even less encouraging, just a stretch of tarmac that seamlessly crumbled into perverse scrubland—useless

43

brush the same washed-out black as the road—that, itself, would perversely crumble from a single touch. Too fragile to hide in. And too flat to hide behind, Revere realized, tightening her grip on her stolen spear.

The only way then was through. The rapid footfalls and obscene yelling behind her was an assurance better than most that going around wasn't an option. Not with this place drenched in enough dust to pick her footprints out with an almost forensic perfection. There was no weather in Hell.

Through was the only way. Besides, she reasoned, the backdoor might be locked—or it could be made of stronger stuff than glass on the front doors. Wasn't worth testing, not at this rate.

Sucking in as deep as a breath she dared with her mask torn away and lying trampled over half a mile up the road, Revere gritted her teeth and raised the butt of her spear to the glass. Judging by the incoming noise—threats of what'd happen if she didn't return the spear and the supplies, promises of what they'd do to her anyway once she did—she had only one shot at this. At escape.

After that, they'd be close enough to start taking their own shots. And while Revere fancied a lot of things in life and, indeed, in afterward, she didn't stop fancying, she didn't fancy another arrow. Or what would follow one.

At first, she steadied the spear's broomstick butt a couple feet away from where the two doors met. But then she readjusted—a serious risk, but one that offered serious rewards. Frowning, movements stiff and sore, weighed down under a rucksack of supplies and satchel of things to eat and a week of sleepless nights, she realized she didn't want to try ram open a door that was padlocked anyway. No, she just needed a hole. An entry point.

A second of silence passed in the deep night. At least, on her side. The three pursuers, two men and one woman, all the standard inimical type that took their new world like a hyper-violent fish to grayscale water, were plenty loud. Revere, though, aimed.

Then the crash. With all her weight behind it, the spear careened through the reinforced glass. Now there was a hole tall enough for a short woman to step through. And without being shredded much either.

Revere tossed the spear through the gap, and then did just that. Dressed as she was—thick denims under thicker winter gear, riding gloves and heavy duty work boots, plus a hood drawn tightly over her an amber face and burnished hair, all of it stained camouflage gray with a dry crust of filth—the jagged mouth of the broken glass door wasn't too deadly. She stepped through it, collected the spear, and then ducked for cover.

Despite the padlock, it seemed, somebody else had beaten her to the place. Maybe they'd put the padlock on, too—although Revere doubted that she was in a world where things rotted, rusted, or decayed correctly anymore. People, at least, just grew colder and, after a while, wouldn't warm up again either. They grew insane, hungry. She wasn't sure what happened with normal food, nonhuman food. She never had enough spare to check.

The convenience store she found herself in had been trashed, enthusiastically so. With practiced eyes piercing through the midnight gloom, she saw a forest of shelves tipped over, their contents long since gone. Empty cans and wrappers scattered the chipped, dusty tiles like mulch of rubbish leaves on the filth-forest floor. And the fridges looked likewise abandoned, and whatever their contents once were, it had all been either drank or curdled for years now. One corner had either been a fireplace, or a toilet. Streaks dark enough to look black in the gloom painted the floor and reached up the wall. In short, the place was a mess.

And outside, her pursuers had arrived. What they promised to do would be far messier than the store at its worst.

But Revere knew messes weren't predictable either. Taking the strap of the spear—once meant for a guitar, or perhaps a rifle—and slinging that over her good shoulder, she pulled her gun. An AMT Hardballer, a M1911 clone that was twice as shiny, cost half as much. Shot decently. No strap required.

Without a doubt, the attackers would barge in through the doorway—the one she'd created. And, no doubt there either, they were all big enough to have to slow down and crack the hole wider first.

After all, she hadn't shot at them when sneaking by their campfire earlier and making off with the first bag of something edible she'd seen. She hadn't shot at them either when half of them gave chase and certainly shot at her. So, Revere hadn't a doubt that they'd simply be expecting their own spear chucked back at them.

Or surrender. Plenty of men proposed surrender to anyone small and feminine enough to be wrestled down easily. And Revere supposed that might be a decent existence for some of them, until cannibalism was on the menu. But she wasn't about to give into anyone she could dupe so easily.

And now, dupe twice over.

From her crouch behind a shelf that had fallen into one of the fridges, Revere checked the gun. Loaded, still. Not enough bullets to shoot down the original eight of them anyway. But, she noted, shoving its magazine back in, more than enough to kill three duped spiky types.

The first man—lanky with off-ochre skin the same color and texture as his leather jacket—set about cracking a bigger hole in the glass with a fire ax. His friend with the facial scars and reddish eyes nodded, took a knee, and raised a hunting crossbow. The woman in the construction helmet nodded to them both and circled around back.

Revere doubted they could see her. The guy with the face like he'd kissed a weedwhacker and then came back for seconds was a good shot, after all. She had the arrow in her shoulder as proof of that. And, her running done for the day—come to think of it— that was beginning to hurt.

The back of her hoodie, denim jacket, and the layers underneath all that were beginning to feel wet. Not hot, not particularly, but a clammy lukewarm sort of wetness that promised serious agony whenever she next found light, the fire needed to heal herself, bring herself back to a mockery of life. Revere didn't grin at the thought—she had other priorities anyway.

She waited until the axman's tool got stuck. Two in the chest followed, with a report like agony slamming a car door. The world went white for a moment, infinitely loud—and when the Hardballer's explosion cleared, the leather man was a corpse on the ground. His tool clattered down a second later, and his friend was too shocked to shoot.

However, Revere wasn't. She'd spent years doing this—day to day, risk to risk, meal to meal, however time worked in Hell—and she'd done it all alone too. In her world, there wasn't time for mourning. There was only her, potential threats, and the means to neutralize them or run away.

And the slowly amplifying pain in her right shoulder promised her that if she ran, she'd be caught. Maybe with their ax, but probably the crossbow. Neutrality was simply not an option.

Ignoring the tinnitus in her ears and the fading spots in her vision, the lone survivor rolled out from under her shelf and caught the scarred man dead in her iron sights. He was knelt down next to his dead friend, and, underneath the burns and the bad surgery, Revere thought his expression might've just been grief. Could've been anger too, however, and his grip was still firm on the crossbow's trigger.

So, she made hers even firmer. But this time, no detonation… Only a click. The hammer fell, it hit the bullet, but the .45 shot didn't fly. The man survived—frosty, distraught, furious, sure, but surviving and murderous. And hearing the sudden snap, spotting a tangle of filthy ginger hair flick into view, he took aim.

And despite what the crossbow had been put through, what horrors its scope had seen and its arrows killed, it didn't misfire. Through the hole in the glass its bolt rocketed. And through Revere's left bicep it crunched.

While she might've been cold enough to shrug off a flesh wound, a point blank shot through bone was something else. Especially after the brief, violent gasp of light the AMT had spat out. Revere was awake enough, human enough, to scream.

The pistol hit the floor. And the man hit reloaded his crossbow while his target scrambled for cover. Her entire torso now alight with agony, the redhead woman limped and tripped and hurried back between the shelves.

And came face to face with the third attacker—the woman in the builder's helmet and ski parka, holding the knives—who had gone around back, and found its door unlocked. The spiky type leered at her opponent, and then leapt forward with a shortsword aimed for the throat, fashionable in lives, worlds, and countries past…

But Revere was shot in the arm, not the leg. Reflexes on maximum, she sidestepped the giddy lunge, and ducked the overeager swipe that followed. And then, her opponent unsteady, opportunity knocked.

The thief answered it with a steel toe to the shin. And got a satisfactorily shocked squawk in response. She followed that with an elbow from her right side, upward into the temple. Still woozy, though, from the gunshot earlier, she missed. Hit the chin instead and felt a canine or two sink into the padding around her forearm.

Regardless, the stunned attacker staggered back, bloodied but definitely not beaten. More cursing, more garbled now, some of it in languages Revere didn't recognize—some that she'd forgotten to speak. All of it profane, detailing where those two knives were going to go.

But the woman had stepped back into her scarred friend's line of sight. And it was dark—it was always dark—and the chaos and the noise and the gunshots hadn't made it easier to pick out friend from thief. Especially since one of the stickers on the knife nut's helmet was, once, a bright orange too.

The crossbowman saw the smeared spot and his hands worked before his mind could order them to still. And, again, he shot true. An arrow burst through her breast a moment later.

Blood pulses quickly followed. Revere clawed up the closer of her knives, and her gun, then slinked back into the shadows. A brief, cautious smile. After all, two down, one to go—and one bullet left. Maybe also a misfire. Or maybe not. Perhaps, the answer to her latest trouble.

Revere was confident the man wouldn't go through the front now—not when his screams had turned from threats of disembowelment and rape to sobs of dismayed horror. Two friends dead. The rest, bound to turn on each-other and starve. And now when his opponent might have another bang waiting for him in the chamber.

No, he'd follow his friend's path around back, doubtless. Try and flank the woman who'd gotten two of his five friends slaughtered. Not like he had anything to come home to. Where was there to go, Revere had used to wonder.

Choices flashed in the thief's mind and they were bad. Slipping back through the hole was baiting an ambush—especially since the thing was now more jagged than ever, she had another arrow's worth of awkward sticking out of her side, and broken glass over tarmac wasn't quiet to step on either.

Similarly, going around could work. It could. But Revere had long since given up on being a gambling woman. Without somebody else's cash to spend, the ideal wasn't as shiny. And wasting her own life existence the guy when he came through the back was an omega lethal suggestion.

But there weren't other options—apart from miracles, and this was Hell. And fixing her gun's jam and hoping the next round would end this fight was a miraculous suggestion. Revere found that out the sore way that a broken arm proved itself useless for racking the Hardballer's slide and holding the chromed gun still while she pried out the dud, unspent bullet.

She sighed, clutched her stolen hunting knife even harder in her offhand, and took position behind the employees-only backdoor. The first inklings of a real plan brewed in her mind, but the footsteps and the enraged ramblings of her opponent grew louder far faster than her ideas could bubble up into something useful.

Possibilities flashed in her head regardless—all of them worse. Unless she got a serious jump on the guy, tore the crossbow out of his hands and followed it up with a cut to kill, the size disadvantage alone would crush her. And that was hoping he didn't swap over to another weapon too, like his friend's ax—now missing from beside the door.

Another deep breath, that was it. Any second and he'd burst through and, unlikely, she'd win. Very unlikely, given her wounded state, she thought. Literally any second. This sore, scratchy breath might be the last one she'd ever take. The dust and the exhaustion tore at her throat as her arm and shoulder throbbed. The dust mixed to mud with what little tears the dehydrated woman had left to cry.

On the one hand, she thought, Susannah Revere had a good run. On the other, that was a lie brighter than fire-red hair in Hell's midnight. Her life had been a mess it wasn't worth it to list. Just as she thought she got lucky, she'd woken up here, and the mess returned. No answers. Zero explanations. Seeing a man pinned down, disemboweled, and his guts eaten raw turned her fast into a shooting first, no questions later kind of girl. But she still had things left to live for, to fight for—a son, somewhere, and, better pressing, no desire to see her corpse defiled by enraged spiky people. They'd start while she still feigned alive.

Revere vowed to go down fighting, and she hoped to hope and back that she wouldn't be going down today.

The footsteps behind had her stopped, and the ranting, the furious promises and screams of death, did too—even under the gunshot buzz in her ears, she was certain of that. Maybe this wasn't a Hell she was stuck in, this garage, not any worse than anything else in this world. Or maybe the man behind the shut door wasn't keen on opening it either. Might get shot, stabbed, or worse, exactly what he planned for her.

Revere didn't care to find out, or eat a human. Hence, why she stole. But right then, her ears were certainly still ringing and that gave her an idea that almost wasn't bad. She had a habit of using guns, and keeping her ears safely bundled under a hood, scarves, masks and, at one point, even a hat. The rest of her stayed under layers of sweaters and coats, any old rag she could find. It all kept the cold and the madness out as well as the sound. The scarred man seemed pretty new to the concept, however, judging by how bad the shots had shocked him earlier. He'd gone half blind from two bullets alone.

Sure, some of that might be the surprise of seeing your best friends die only inches away. But her life was on the line now, and Revere was willing to bet it that the guy's hearing wasn't too great. And that he was confident she had a working round left in her gun, one at least. After all, she'd shot two earlier, to kill one man.

So, Revere stood up, knife still in hand, and, very carefully, around all the trash, the decay, the crumbling dust, she stepped away from the door.

No reaction. So, she did it again—and kept doing it until she was in the center of the room. Then, looking at the door, the hole in it, and what was left of her chances, she gathered everything she had left in the tank. All those years of white-knuckled, red-blooded survival, the horror and the evil and the constant night and endless death, her new life, the tank itself.

Revere took it all in, took one last look at the door and the man in the standoff behind it—she ran.

Let   the   night   have   her.

Ruby Dagger

Or the Thoughts of a regretful thief.

By Roman Anthony

I T has been a month since I found that dagger. That God-**damned** dagger.

It started with chickens, but then even an entire flock wasn't enough. I moved to cows, and that—at first—seemed to calm it. Again, it only seemed to, because within days before the light turned to night I had to sate its bloodlust again. And again. And again.

I hadn't planned for this. I had never even wanted to take anything. I just needed shelter from the foul weather that night.

It first caught my eyes in the ancient count's abode, as it shined brightly as it stuck out of his skeleton. I couldn't help myself; sparkly things are always attractive. When I saw the faded, translucent vermillion gemstone it was made of... It just *called* to me. I never thought about keeping it—the price it'd fetch would pay for a proper horse, perhaps even a small cottage!

How could I have been so *foolish* to be able make a mistake this bad? Was it when I decided that sleeping in the stables wasn't enough, and to explore and rummage through that abandoned manor? No, perhaps it was before all that. Perhaps I should have just followed mother's advice, just apprenticed to a tailor, just marry the baker's daughter. Her flame-red hair had always enamoured me anyway, and we could have lived a quiet life in that quiet little hamlet. A quiet and boring life.

No, that was never going to happen.

No, I guess the real mistake was the moment I took that wench to my room and had thrust that accursed dagger into her beating, gushing, excited little heart. And as the light faded from her eyes, the blade's colour returned to its true colour; a bright blood-red ruby.

And now here I am, brooding on my rented bed in a village I didn't even want to be in, let alone for a whole damned month. Even selling the dagger to some itinerant peddler didn't free me. The hawker nearly signed away his soul for it, so I guess he had never seen a weapon so gorgeous either? A 'blade' cut from a single piece of gemstone—although both of us couldn't identify it for sure—, sharpened and compressed until its edges were sharper than razors, on a vaguely blued yet obviously gold crossguard, and a hilt of ivory inscribed with wrong patterns in even more gold… At the very least, whoever made this little shank was a master craftsman.

But the cursed bloodlust didn't leave me, leaving me with no choice. I **just had** to buy it **back** before he got too far. But alas, it seemed he was gone as well. So I had to cure him from it. Now the coin he had on him is paying for my stay here. This isn't even a proper inn, just a ramshackle tavern that rented their own bedroom away once I'd lightened my—sorry, his—coinpurse.

But I have to wonder, was the old dead count its creator and master, or its victim? Hell's bells, perhaps he was both! He was known as a hermit to his subjects, with no family or known progeny. Perhaps he was a student of the occult? Cutting a solid gemstone into a dagger, infusing it with dark powers rejected by the Lord Above…

Did he plunge his cursed dagger into his own heart, out of guilt of murdering all his family and servants? Or did the lack of close-by would-be victims leave him with no other choice?

I know now that this blood-cursed dagger doesn't allow one their own mind. That moment I took it out between those ribs… I felt its malevolence forced upon me. The count must've felt the same I guess. It matters not, not anymore. The dagger—and his curse—is mine now.

A knock on the door.

I guess it must be the tavernkeep's daughter bringing me my ale and stew. Oh, how beautiful she is, I half-dreamed of asking if she came with the room! She caught my eyes the moment I walked in this place. Her rosy-red cheeks, her exposed milky skin just above her chest…

She's just fine. Yesss. She's just what I needed.

Saccharine

By Amousai

ATOP a mountain range of green overlooking greener valleys, lie a temple shrouded in red where old monks and their young acolytes live and enrich themselves and others who should come. For every man and boy whose heads were shaved alike was an acolyte who was tasked to sweep the temple's entrance ground on that eventful day. Of almost fifty heads to count, only the eyes on his would not see the cause of the temple's condemnation and the subsequent effect of a series of undefinable political assassination for those local officials who had gotten involved.

It was a sweltering summer day where the blossomed leaves of the cherished ginkgo trees had made him able to cool off. The ground he was sweeping looked practically clean to anyone else, but he was still tasked to do so for it was more of a matter of discipline than literal cleanliness. His sweeping was slow but rhythmical for his mind had directed his hands and gaze to be steady. So lowered was his gaze that the neck strain he had to endure wouldn't last long for anyone untrained. Although the torii gate had poured in crowds of people with more coming, he hadn't made the mistake of sweeping dust to the right and twigs and leaves to the left. They were where they belonged like the sparrows tweeting from the tree branches. But suddenly, something startled the sparrows and they flew away exiting through the torii. The crowds were audibly amazed and excited to see such a wonderful sight of flight. Some even went down to their knees praying, for a number of the local deities had been told throughout folk legends to have taken utmost the appearances of various birds.

The acolyte lost for a split second his concentration as he had given the sparrows and their tweeting a home in his mind. This he had done because he had been taught that the love and appreciation nature isn't perverse. So he loved and appreciated nature as they come for rather than be sought after by the pious of the temple. Man on the other hand – especially woman – would be the bane of their existence if cared for. Although every entering acolytes were to learn about it very early on, it was not an uncommon rumor-of-the-day for an acolyte or two to overhear the drunken stupors of the senior monks telling tales of women and their habitation. Though every rumor shared similar traits and went away as quickly as the previous one, the habitation of those women and their elusive, exotic habitats never failed to perk the ears of the living space residents. Unlike tales of rich feasts and their quenching drinks, as those experienced in them became shunned for speaking more of this vice of others.

Even though his concentration had only been lost for a split second, specks of dust had been swept to the left for a single twig had been casted to the right, collecting more dust the longer it would take for him to react. So he set his broom to sweep the two back to where they belonged but the broom fought him. Where he wanted to sweep, it would go in the opposite direction. He couldn't get in control as no matter how much he cleansed his mind, the magical annoyance wasn't about to dispel. He was about to point and blame the sun or the ginkgo's leaves, whichever metaphysically justifiable to lash out on. As he was making sure that neither the sun nor the ginkgo trees had moved in magical manners as his broom did, he saw that it was black.

An imperfect triangular-shaped blackness in between two paleness almost as bright as the sun yet the shadows uncovered caving upward veiled through-and-through any other means of the black's truth. In a time felt much faster than the split of a second, it was gone. Replaced by an encompassing whiteness which somehow blended into the crowds whose colors amongst many had shades nowhere near the white that the black had encompassed. The acolyte saw neither the face of the owning subject nor the crowds'. Somehow, they all turned theirs to all sides but where he and that person were. Like subjects of the dramas inside the greatest paintings, dramatically unable to face their dramas. When at last he was able to throw his head up and see that both the sun and the ginkgo's leaves hadn't magically moved. But the sun had somehow shone so great that he was blinded in an instant as if the leaves meant to act as shields were as uncooperative as the broom meant to clean.

The acolyte would then unmistakably drop his broom. Mistakably, however, was the sound of the broom hitting the stones of the grounds sounding far louder than anyone had expected. Making heads around the crowds turn toward where the boy was standing. Those gathered closest in front of him were heard murmuring about a shaking feeling beneath their feet, which was then felt a few seconds after from one side of the crowd to another, ending with many in the crowds chattering much louder than they should be. The acolyte was the sole authority amongst less than five combined teachers responsible for the crowds of touring high school students. While the boys can laugh the weird situation off, a sizable number of girls immediately panicked and went off further into the temple, causing one teacher to chase after them which soon turned into two as those highschool boys weren't about to miss out on anything and nothing at the same time.

Being left with an even fewer number of responsible adults

with many of the teenagers still wandering here-and-there wanting to do what the others did, the acolyte aptly walked away to where his broom was. Shutting off the teachers-students dilemma to fill his mind with the prayers still chanted out-and-away from the main temple. Their words coupled with the arrangements of the instruments should have filled him who was coming back under the ginkgos' guise with the harmony of rightfulness. Yet, on every other chant and tunes, the melodious prayers were assailed by disharmony of clandestine malignancy. It was less knowledge and more gut feeling which made him know so. So he swept in anxiousness, unable to bring the dust, twigs, and leaves to where they should be without repeating at least two times. And he pushed his neck and head back down, now with less consecration and more embarrassment. That was until, not even the sound of his geta clacking heard and closing in, was the frog-smiled *oshō*.

His hefty body vesseling a mind trained for purity allowed the wind to treat him as light as a sheet of paper. He had the wind help him brush his robe softly up so that it touched against the acolyte's thigh. The ticklish acolyte knew very well the *oshō* firm playfulness, so he stood straight, bowed, and waited with an open heart for his conviction. The *oshō* curtained the side of his head then cupped his ear before pointing toward where the visitor's restrooms were. So the acolyte began walking there without his broom, without his head moving from where the *oshō* had gotten it glued.

Dedicated for the visitors as restrooms were a structure simply rectangular built near an outskirt of one of the temple's storage areas. It was meant to not blend with the rest, not to overtake the arrangement of the temple's grounds and its buildings. Fortunately for the acolyte, visitors of a temple as remote as theirs were known to have made the journey generally not out of the baseness of the spectacles of tourism. As carefully maintained as the temples were in the big cities, the acolyte's own experiences and hearsays suggested that even the restrooms of the holiest of all places could invite miscreants unthinkable. So he remembered the contrast of being at lovely Kyoto's Kinkaku-ji, chasing after a rabbit who hopped after gardens and ponds, finally caught but died after three days because her lungs were filled by smokers' smokes entrapped inside the west men's restroom against the nothingness that he hadn't known happened at his temple.

It was blasphemous for the acolyte to think that just as he was cleaning, he undoubtedly caught a whiff of smoke coming from outside. Same smell meant the same brand and all of the smokers responsible for the indirect death of Kinkaku-ji's beloved rabbit. He was to be the first person to intercept the first tainting of their restrooms of nothingness. As he expected, the suspects had come from amongst the students of the visiting crowds. Unexpected was how they carried themselves, wildly different from the other girls.

Thoughtful abandonment of modesty and conformity fashioned the two of them. Pragmatically speaking, they would endure the heat a lot better than others, but it should be left to nature to endow shade before the imperfection of one's ingenuity. When the acolyte asked them to stop, they mimicked his manners with pregnant exaggeration that made certain areas of their bodies sway rashly without the wind picking them up. With both physical and mental visions closed, the acolyte bent down the dirt though he was still teased and laughed at and gathered as much as possible in his hands fallen leaves that weren't coarse and dirty. It was a wild but welcomed idea if one understands the order to which he belonged as he proceeded to shove those leaves inside the crevices of the girls' exposed tops.

Like him, they were ticklish. In congruent to their appropriate protests were giggles of thinly-veiled annoyance, anger, and caution all mixed into one. With each passing seconds grew doubt in the acolyte's heart whether the method was ever tested to be true. Whether some degenerate times ago had planted a false seed which still bloomed to his generation and further. And so he felt like a degenerate for having failed to get it done quickly and more so when the point between the leaves and bare flesh was accidentally reached by his hand. One of the girls screamed and he wanted to as well. It was subsequently granted, yet, it was because the sun had shone right again into his eyes.

A few hours later he would then tell the boy of gangled ears who spoke little for his lips looked permanently chapped, the situation he found himself waking up to, for he would be able to tell anyone everything, whether believed or not, but this one no more. He had woken up with his eyes, nose, lips, and ears where they belonged; of the same face as well as voice. But the rest of his body could neither be seen nor felt and he could only see forward where a buried eye met his eyes. The buried eye, enmeshed against a wall of flesh which flexing and relaxing implied its aliveness. It spoke with mouth unknown, but the acolyte who remembered seeing where his head was was like a mouth later told his listener that he was simply inside one. Though that gangling-eared boy could offer a few understanding that the acolyte couldn't, he spoke naught of what he might have known of, only smacking that chapped lips once in a while to both wet it and confirm to the acolyte that he was still listening. So what was known of the buried eye, walls of flesh, and mouth unknown was what it wanted to tell the acolyte was buried far deeper – than the buried eye – and worse by cries that sounded to be produced by children. Even the buried eye seemed to look progressively distressed as it continued to serve as their mouthpiece. Instantaneously when the verbal transmission ended, a torrent of fetid thick white liquid coupled with the most putrid of all blood gushed into the forcibly opening eyes, ears, nose, and mouth of the poor acolyte. And as he drowned, he felt plucked several sets of hands that dropped him down the ground and cleaned his eyes so that he can see that he can still see the sun but left his ears, nose, and mouth to fend off their master's ongoing liquid torments.

He cried himself to a river and more as he had kept running until his legs had almost given up for he was deep in the woods unable to find any indication of the temple's redness in the distance, but fortunate enough to end up by a river tranquil. He thanked Buddha through thousands of pronounced words with the help of the river's refreshing cold water, never letting his lips and mouth run dry. And as he had dirtied the river's clarity with red and white and apologized for it, he saw an image of a boy sitting on the other side. Before he was able to call out for him, the boy had leapt through stones to where he was, asking why he had done that to the river. Although he had yet to tell him, they were eventually able to meet each other at a peaceful point. The boy whom the acolyte then saw wasn't Japanese, was distinguishable for his gangling ears, and latter, his permanently chapped lips to which he found out when the boy, consuming more water than he, for he couldn't stand the heat more, never was rid of his chapping.

They soon went on a walk together because the gangling-eared boy claimed that he was a guest of the temple under the command of his honorable master and mistress who had sent him away to fetch water. When asked why must he found himself all the way deep in the woods, he only professed that it wasn't up to him to question their specifics; for in the past when servants began to question themselves and others too much, they never failed to fail their given tasks. The acolyte lightheartedly joked that he hoped his venial tainting hadn't made their way to the boy's vessel; to which the boy gave a silent refusal, like when he was offered help to carry the thing.

In about less than an hour that they took to arrive back at the temple, for the gangling-eared boy was able to gracefully trace the steps he took even though he was a mere visitor, he let the acolyte have the privilege of knowing his "name". He told him he was an eunuch, but not in Japanese. The acolyte, who spoke not the language but didn't want to offend he who had made the effort to speak his, came to pronounce his "name" as □*unu*. For the rest of their life, neither the acolyte nor the gangling-eared boy would know the name of the latter person, for like the former Buddhist who shouldn't seek trifle, it was in a eunuch's best interest to follow so.

Having escorted the acolyte back, □*unu* went toward his

accommodation. The acolyte too had planned to immediately go back to his post despite what had just recently happened. Much of a rest seemed not to be a privilege grantable to either the two, as the acolyte's steps were stopped when ☐unu, speaking for the loudest he would ever be heard for him, called out. Though it was a short call, the acolyte took notice of how specially feminine he sounded. An unnaturally splendid mezzo-soprano that no such men could naturally have. Even the women-men of Thailand whom the acolyte had the pleasure to see several times for their kinds if coming in purity to temples' grounds, must be respected as others honored, reached in their most ardent cries of prayers no pitch as high as ☐unu. The acolyte wondered how peculiar it was how many feminine factors, crude or good, had gone his way throughout the day as he walked. Coming out and standing beside ☐unu then was an old monk who took the boy into a conversation with him. ☐unu turned toward the man and the acolyte saw onto his back a chest tightly strapped.

The small talk stopped when the acolyte joined. He was given the command to once again become ☐unu's companion. His master and mistress had gone out and needed to be fetched, and the timing couldn't be more perfect now that their servant had fulfilled everything they needed; details unknown. Where they would go would be the other side of the valleys, the path less trod by most but fallen men and women. The smallest of sinners to the biggest, such as the retiree farmers turn daytime gamblers to the suits responsible for building such outlets. No road from the north, which didn't touch their side of the valleys, was ever built to connect them with the rest. But with times and ages that had come, of Japan belonging as one, those from the south and the west broke the safeguarded seal. Nevertheless, the unenthusiastic outsider must roll with his role, and he who lived the land shan't then desire excuses. So the latter shall prepare to chamber his body, heart, and mind; while the former need not any. And they went with their feet for what would they say if they saw the Buddhist and the lowly servant drive into the maw of the other side of the valleys.

They strained their bodies arduously against roads formed of ever changing directions accompanied by the furious heightened swelter of noon's summer sun. The moment when they had been passed by several cars to find that the road they were going to had lined up throughout its sides bamboos and spring trees, of Japanese and occidental, made to be bloomed artificially, even as everywhere around them nature-breed floras had painted the landscapes in accordance to what the valleys and mountain ranges should. The acolyte walked straight and the eunuch walked with a hunched back toward the loathsome gate those ill-fitting planters protected. And as the acolyte walked through the numerous garish knickknacks curtaining it, the fondles they had on his skin made him shudder for it was rather the sounds they made, practically the same as the jangling of sundry braces and necklaces adorning those two grotesque high school girls; whom fates he would never know had ended grotesque and buried near the body of that river by the eunuch. Done in a Christian manner for he never grasped learning that the saying goes "born Shinto, marry Christian, die Buddhist," and he, as with other topics, never had it conversed with the acolyte, but not out of respect for Buddhism and their followers.

Whereas filling throughout the valleys excellent mountain's breeze heralded by many, to the extension of the people of capital Tokyo, as being their keys for the prolongation of their already long healthy lives, the suffocating air inside the valley's mystery was a textbook antithesis of it. Perfumes of many scents made clear to must have been made garishly cheap, by un-delicate hands, without care to befriend one profile to another. And the excessiveness to which they have been doused throughout every inches of the enigmatic juncture could never dissipate for as strangely artificial were the stones they had paving their roads, stranger was the ceiling unseen from outside but clear to the eyes once inside trapping everything, dead or alive, in its architectural decree. Lost in trances were the acolyte and the eunuch that their steps stumbled like the heaviest of drunks, and would fall like one they would have had their arms weren't woven in the caresses of two ladies; for each arms. Wherever the four of them would spin their eyes to where they might follow the eunuch's direction, luminous redness would burn so bright their meddlesome retinas. But brightness was the brilliance of that mysterious place, so the mystifying thrill of uncovering what and why lured the acolyte and the eunuch to revel in the pain and pleasure. How delightfully depraved was their reward for beyond the discernible neon lights – the hosts of those lights – they were to then be able to read Japanese, Chinese, and foreign characters, either isolated or altogether, governed to spell obscenities. Though the acolyte should realize later on when it was too late, those words shall be borne to live and die as sacredly profound as mantras that had shaken him to his core on the rarest of occasions he never wished to repeat. But so powerless, as intended, should be once he carelessly or meticulously entered that heart of mystery, so after many passed streets, corners, men, women, visions, and sounds; of the hellish, miscreants, and perverted, was a set of stairs climbed, a door and window shut, and a robe as well as a kimono doffed. Their perspiring sweats should be released now that copulation should be bestowed between the two unopposed. And let it be known that the eunuch, who had dismissed his companion back to where she unabashedly belonged, had procured from the nearby wardrobe a shamisen of which his roughed hands had become so sensitive that the ill attempt he had shamelessly started with came to seamlessly illustrate sounds of distant Arab followed by a singing coming from his same chapped lips that no men, women, nor angels could ever rival, yet were able to be savored by a single pair of man or woman whom coarseness of gripes and moans had blocked their ears from the springing arabesque.

When the eunuch's gangling ears had finished dancing to his oriental-homed tunes, the woman whom the acolyte was with would have finished as well. She was to be paid a sack full of faraway gems and jewels and added coins in exchange for a strip of her robe cut, perfumed, and clothed around the acolyte's resting pelvis. She went out only after she had the help of the house's madam to shave her head. To which she would be proud as the act signified another win for their belief that the opposite attracts; to the dismaying dismissal of the monks' teaching from the other side of her valleys. Curious onlookers loudly cheered and clapped their hands as she made her ways all-around and everywhere. The eunuch soon disappeared as the crowds' loudness began to pierce the walls of the bedroom, and more importantly, amongst the first of the crowds to cheer and clap were heard beyond doubt his master and mistress'.

The liveliness which had woken up the acolyte had almost ended in a tragedy as in his unfully awoken state, he had rolled around the room and knocked the eunuch's chest to almost crush his head. His heart was racing but noticeably weaker than it would usually be despite what had just happened. He didn't fret about it for too long, for his head which had been filled with so many memories yet so little clarity put him in a state where not even one thought could be clearly processed. Yet he still forced himself up only to see in the mirror his body in an almost complete nudity. Tracing down from his well-endowed yet fatigued physics were stains of wines and liquors alike. Their colors had darkened with the room dimness like blood alike. And their musks shalt mix with the damp muskiness of others' insidiousness, left insidious. So the acolyte took a hasty leave for he was afraid of the creeping remembrance of his bodiless head.

Out in the streets that were as fragrant as before, the acolyte then unaffected was able to take in better what he was seeing and listening for the worse. Fiends and minxes well dwelled in the creeps of darkened grounds in wicked chattering, and in deeper darker shades would be where they went worse. Nothing pleasant was in what they engage and exchange in, except for the pleasantries they engage and exchange before they move on to their dealings deemed more important. Nevertheless, even only in partial, the arrays of darkness had at least allowed the acolyte's eyes to not know, but the ears couldn't be closed off as entirely as the eyes. Despite how quickly he could move throughout streets, alleys, and corners, the ears would continue to dirty themselves with stories that the eyes couldn't help at times be kept untold. In the end, he narrowed his ears and eyes and with much difficulty stumbled himself to an exit.

Amidst the sprightliness of drunkards, gamblers, harlots, and servants in brothels, inns, and card houses alike would be sung rowdily for days to come about the acolyte's journey inside-out. For never had neither monk nor acolyte made the treacherous journey to that other side of the valley and went in with such frolic to just come out with much remorse. Varying brothels bid on the two girls who were capable of seducing the acolyte and the eunuch, and while the former was guaranteed better living conditions, the latter was deemed a fraud when they found out what the name ⬜*unu* actually meant. Yet, she would found herself years later thanking profusely that stranger for having led her to an honest life tending lands for lovely fruits and vegetables, while her colleague would live and die in the same mysterious heart of that other side of the valley, failed to hold onto her acclamation and more once she turned into her own madam. For that place was and would always be blind and deaf to anything and everything outside of its own decadent dogma.

Chasing after the acolyte who had managed to get out was a servant girl who was considerate enough to drag by herself the chest her hirers thought was his. The acolyte wondered how such a small girl was able to carry such a thing considering that she looked healthier and fuller than the eunuch. When he picked it up for himself did he realize that it was empty. The servant girl too didn't know where the content went. Only that the madam she worked under bought it after it had been emptied, was figuring out where to put it by her establishment, only to be told by a handsome foreigner in blonde a tall tale of an ancient Shinto curse. So, knowing that a passing Buddhist acolyte just made a name for himself, the foreigner made her agree that it was the best course of action to pass it down to him. As the acolyte was weighing in the decision of coming back in, armed with the tall tale passed down from the foreigner, to the madam, to the girl, and finally him to frighten the opportunistic thief. But then, a foreigner fitting the servant girl's description walked into the scene.

Surpassing the acolyte's expectation, the handsomeness of the alluded was realized down the rich luster of his blonde hair, a face etched into through-and-through into bewitching smoothness. Sharp eyes, nose, and lips planted onto that smooth surface with the sharpness of the eyes being the most luxuriant for it shall be used as the beginning point of captivation. Only when a subject longingly dared address him after his eyes had cut theirs would they see how light would brighten the tip of his nose; and that shall possess them to pass on to his slyly smiling lips, and lastly, the aroma of tulip would then fill the air between he and the subject he let speak with him. In the case between him and the acolyte, the former would be full of laughs and humors and the latter, with eyes casted down, sparingly said anything; their conversation went nowhere.

Mending the awkwardness of the two were three of the man's companions; the eunuch, a woman looking like him, and an old man sharp in suit. It was the woman who pointed to the chest belonging to her and instructed her servants to take it from the acolyte's hands. The foreigner in blonde went into a surprise and turned toward her side alongside the eunuch and the old man. They spoke without hush for it was in their foreign tongue. They were expressive yet cryptic and they seemed to be heard talking only a few sentences before erupting into a laugh together, save the eunuch and the old man. The acolyte saw the woman turning to him, pointing somewhere around his stomach. He was able to put the pieces together when he felt in velveteen feel, the wrapped cloth that had escaped him in the darkness of that room. Confused he was on what to do until the eunuch shook his hand at him, telling him to leave it be.

As the sun had been going west and more, the acolyte was convinced to go with the group of foreigners to return to the temple. They drove in a limousine helmed by the old man. The acolyte and the eunuch were saved in a cramped space by the back while the latter's master and mistress were to be pampered in the middle with cushions of velours for their back and glasses of sparkling champagne for their hands with the blowing mountain wind refreshing their faces. They would go between drinking and touching and making rumbling of the prone to crashing cars. Then, lay the woman, the mistress, by her beloved chest that in some such way was gleaming with gems of many gamuts from the most radiant topazes to blazing rubies despite never having looked to be more than an old yet ornate chest before. Now, to be in touch with her pale silky skin had further made, somehow, a coalescent between her made bare back and the dead object completing itself with her, or was it the other way around? And the acolyte stared in marvel for what was seeing one more thing beyond his comprehension? Then he felt his grip instinctively tighten against the seat in front, and his mouth salivating, dropping against those leathers. Yet, sat still did the eunuch while the acolyte was left to fend for his behooving acting. The acolyte's eyes locked with the eunuch's master, who then still laughed when his sharp eyes cut into the acolyte's, who threw them down just to see the kisses and caresses that foreign body openly invited.

Unlike then, in an excuse of uncalled for trance, was the entrapment that caught onto the acolyte. So then, inside that limousine, was it being played once again, without the smoke screen of illusion. So the eunuch and the old man – more accurately, their butler – had yet to come meddling, until suddenly a womanly scream was heard followed by a loud thud. The acolyte fell from the back to the master's lap and he grabbed onto the mistress' chest on his way down. Almost all of the passenger weights went to the right, and as the limousine was making a sharp turn to the left, came crashing down everything and everyone else in that car down a steep valley.

Awoken the acolyte to not even the slightest bit of scratch and everyone else except the eunuch's mistress unconscious while in front of them, yet not touching them, the limousine ablaze and its flame dancing from tree to tree. Strangely being the only one that can save her, he dragged his ever so strangely energized body to her. But, as he picked her up, slowly turned the dress and jewelries she adorned herself in into specks of dust; realized to be gold. And her former attire turned gold dust flew into the fiery spectacle. And came spewing from that infernal maw a bunny as white as Hokkaido's snow. The rabbit hopped aloof and passed the disastrous scene into a path behind the acolyte and the nude lady to the darkness unfitting its fur. Yet, it noticed itself being left alone, so it came back, looked at the acolyte, and threw itself back into the fire. The acolyte screamed but it was too late but then came spewing out two more bunnies. One stayed by his side while the other took the path beforehand. As the other had gone unseen, the one who stayed understanding how glued the acolyte still was, threw itself back into the fire. And the acolyte screamed, and it repeated. The bunnies multiplied in two everytime and the acolyte saw and smelled many charred bunnies.

After a while of the unstopping oddness, the acolyte was able to remind himself that he wasn't safe yet. He hightailed it out with the woman in his hand and the bunnies on his tail. By then, she had gone completely naked and he felt wrongful. But, as wrongful as he felt, even more confused was he to once again be lost in the woods. He had run everywhere just to end up in a circle infested with the danger of endangering those innocent bunnies. It didn't matter how little he wanted to give up, his body did by itself at the end.

Slumped by a mound which he would never find out burying underneath two bodies of familiar faces, the acolyte stuck his eyes up to the sky. He didn't dare look down for his hazy memories slowly coming into clarity were warning him not to dare it. Alas, a voice called and a hand pulled, and so he looked underneath and though he was enveloped in the dark, mailed away were those darkness. And from his mouth he started salivating, and more so once the hand pulled him closer that his coarse face felt the softness of her breasts and she spoke in cries of a broken Japanese seemingly saying brother. Stupidly he thought he was the one, and so he attested her deliriousness. In his last remembrances were the bunnies crowding them, fighting for the motherly fountain, but only he was quenched of his defeat of thirst and hunger. And when it had dried up, had gone her body from flesh and bone to specks of dust. Thought perhaps to be gold like her dress and jewels, but so coarse were they, coarser than his coarsest palm that he swatted them away and they made into lights instead. So bright and beautiful were those lights that he forgot her to follow them. And he hiked and trod without diminishing strength until he saw at a distance closer than he expected the red temple's *sanmon*.

The bunnies had dispersed everywhere and anywhere but the temple's grounds. The acolyte himself walked past the last tour bus and a number of locals visiting. He traded evening greetings with them but maintained his distance until he was sure he had made it back to his dorm, passing no one else on his way.

The moment he had gotten to his bed was the moment where came swarming in other acolytes. Both parties were surprised to see each other and the latter began to question the former where he had been all day. But they simply didn't give him a moment to properly answer them as they became rowdy once someone mentioned smelling something peculiar. The loudest and bluntest in the room described it as the aroma of trashiness; ones which had made troublesome yet promising acolytes exiled and shuddered the thinking of the remaining pious ones. About a half of them stayed quiet or chattering in low voices by the corner while the other half pressed on the acolyte. Holding him and unrobing him layer-by-layer, and that loudest and bluntest one from before would almost see that cloth around his waist had it not been for the sudden deafening shrieks of a murder of crows.

From the open window, flew in while still shrieking as deafening as possible those murder of crows. Pecking and taking apart everyone's robes apart, they were left fighting the inexplicable chaos with neither help nor escape possible. Indubitable chaos rose worse when one person had gotten their manhood pecked, followed by another, and everyone else soon were struck the same way. A room full of nude concoctions brewed right after with more than expected on the floor and corners; bodies stretched distorted by freshly gaped wounds made ache through the coating of drowning fallen tears. Several crows did fall, almost equaling the number of the fallen acolytes, but they were ever agile and ferocious. So left the last three crows almost unharmed, their beaks the bloodiest of them all, they met together their grimy wings and took flying a poor poor youngest acolyte of them all.

The loathsome depths of the night unpierced for all naked eyes, had brought down the curtain for the flight of the crows and their victim. It went by unnoticed for quite a while as almost everyone had been howling and still. And in their shivers, they had come to be gutless, therefore their unreliability made them had to be left alone while the relatively unscathed acolyte took a lionhearted flight into the awaiting abnormal night. Just a split second before the doors were torn down and old monks came pouring in.

The three crows left cried loudly in both mourning and triumph as they flew with belly-fulls of blood and meat. Close where they to be as near and as amongst the forest's trees as if mocking the acolyte who was chasing after them. Each passing seconds made it unclear if their victim would still make it out alive, especially when came raining down blood in one swift instance, almost hitting and blinding the chasing acolyte. He was ever at full speed with an equally full conviction against himself yet lack of light for his sights, and surfaces for his hands and feet hindered how capable he was in matching the crows and their domain of utter vast skies. Still he kept running and hurting even when the forest had torn apart his robe to leave him in complete bondage to her elements.

The unforeseen coldness of the night had left his body feeling frozen, dejecting the sliver of morale he had left to atone his inconceivable sins. He was frightened of the horror of dying impurely by nature's uninviting hours; far from the righteous prayers he deserved hearing, far from the atonement he deserved conceiving. Leaning by a tree, covering himself as he could conceive by leaves and twigs as exactly coldened. He sought and failed in the building of a fire. His strength would diminish soon in allness.

Came then in suddenness from the bellow of the night's murkiness, eleven mouth speaking and their eleven pair of limbs cringing. Each of them was erect more than the tallest of trees' shades yet despite those statures, they hadn't brought with them destruction upon the forest's livings. Their limbs too danced macabre yet in passing of any materials they came in contact with. And so they kept in repeat their animations until came to be viewed by the acolyte, the eleven faces becoming one and the limbs too resting as one at last. Through eleven mouths awaited, the governing one spoke of the who that had dared to tread which they deemed theirs. Accompanied in the name of Buddha, the acolyte introduced himself in a manner which pleased the ancient grotesqueness. They gave him a new set of robes tailored from excesses of gores; to which he wore with clandestine agony of terror for were it animals, men, or worse which contributed to its creation. Alas, it was far warmer than he expected and he soon forgot its dubious origin. Continued in question of what the acolyte sought was his answer of the acquaintance taken by the crows. To this, eleven boisterous laughs blared; and they asked him once again just for him to give the same answer. And they continued laughing and repeating until they had extracted all of the humors never understood by the left-out acolyte. The hand of one craned again into twenty-two and in mere seconds, all of those had been protracted to touch an entrance of a far far distant cave dwelling. The acolyte meekly blurted the impossibility of making the trip-and-back alive to which the masked ears of the ancient picked up. Cowered the acolyte as it tears itself back into eleven with looks of substantial worseness. The ten offspring each spoke of a way for him to succeed, with the last, first, one only confirming what the tens suggested. Bitter was the taste in his mouth to be given the suggestion of conspiring with such folks, but at the same time, he had known that he had fallen far from the Buddha's grace.

So he accepted. The robe of gores rattled, crawled, and

consummated his very own fleshes. Spoke one of the face of eyes and nose squashed, teeths missing and rearranged, and skins slitted; of pig-like voice, the status of his failure. For let it be known to the fleshes unseen, incapable of lies, their rot should come fulfilled by sunrise. Wide awake was the acolyte's eyes as his mouth vomited blood yet his constitution as a whole didn't feel defied. In contrast, in edifying his perilous journey had been tasked for him a steed of a horse disfigured. Worry not, they told him, for she was the nimblest of them all. With an empty guts slowly but surely stricken by lecherous hexes, the discomfort of transport and attire queer, and one of the eleven capsuled in riddle requirement fulfilled in the form of the velveteen cloth he had long forgotten been around his waist; the acolyte set forth against nature's cold but not the cold of spirits' guiles.

His steed kept strangely neighing around an area of the forest insurmountable to tell the difference from anywhere else for the opulent night's stars nought penetrate through the forest's umbra. Where the horse fell was crucial but never would the acolyte realize it for he was too busy running away; away from the robe of gores profuse twitching once they were there. Once again, by those two mounds overshadowing their shallow burial grounds would be the then tasted-by-worms bodies of the two high school girls from that morning. Two times already had the acolyte uncovered their fates; two times already he had failed without a chance for a third. Therefore, the only thing the acolyte found on his way was the same river he first met the eunuch; to which he briefly had a moment to wash, drink, and remember he who had disappeared.

As the acolyte made his way up once again and for the last time to the temple, he shall never see the trickery pulled on him. Ten riddles left incomplete yet the rot kept consuming. Imperceivable were the pains they gave; compounded in what felt by the thousands. By the sliver of the utmost forbearance was the acolyte able to drag himself by the steps toward the temple's entrance. Came crashing in the aglow of lights so luminously inviting that he felt his body turning absolutely lithe and he soon walked – not dragged – himself up until the stairs of the main temple. Appealing from somewhere deep inside was a womanly voice, naught fought for control by any other, for him to follow. Alas, he thought he knew more than to believe the first outright claim of help or comfort, so he outright threw his head another direction away. Nevermore would such a venal episode happen or end like his who saw through either unaccounted or deliberate design felted on temple's ground the consummation of bodies. The ancient grotesqueness came in lightspeed to reveal the blind they had thought veiled them; then they all laughed. And the acolyte let out such a saccharine scream that he became unaware of the transition of his pitch due to the eunuch – of shadows abiding – castrated him. And those accursed siblings and their steadfast servants turned to the coarsest of dusts dyed yellow, flew into the foredoomed night, never to be caught unlike the piteous   acolyte.

The Trees

By Donovan Hall

I don't like the trees. They kill people, and no one can really explain why. They don't kill all the time. Just some people, sometimes. But still, if your fridge had just a 1 and 1000 chance of crushing you in your sleep, you'd probably think twice about locking your kitchen at night. So, when my sister rang my up about Jason's big 30th, I wanted to tell her no. Jason lived in the countryside, where the trees were.

"I've been planning this dinner party all month!" she said over the phone.

"Why couldn't you have invited Jason downtown. We could have it at your place, or mine, even."

"You know neither of our spots is big enough to host all his friends. Jason's new house is big. I wanna take advantage of the space. So, you comin' or not?"

"All those *trees* out there though."

"Don't you get tired being paranoid all the time. The trees are fine. I've been out there before and they leave me alone just fine."

I sighed. If I bailed, Carla would never let me hear the end of it, no matter what the excuse. I agreed, hung up, and closed my laptop. It was already past noon. If I was gonna get there before dark, I'd have to leave now.

I put on some decent clothes, locked my apartment door, and headed down to the parking garage. The road out of town took me past Rose Park. I gave it a few glances as I drove past. It was funny, since I never really noticed the trees there before. They were chill, and everyone just assumed they knew how to behave. You almost never heard of one of them going off and killing anybody in a city. Maybe because they'd be too easy to track down. Trees knew better. They knew they could hide in numbers out beyond the city. And now that I was heading in that direction, I guess I just started seeing every piece of foliage a bit differently.

The tension crept through my spine as the skyscrapers and tower blocks began to disappear behind me to give way to the vast, monotonous, openness of the suburbs, and then to wretched tracks of trees and fields. The countryside in all its terror. I turned on the radio to calm my nerves. It didn't help.

"*At 9:30 PM last night,*" the news reporter began, "*a man was killed while jogging in Deer Grove. Police say that he was slain by a belligerent tree.*"

"Deer Grove…" I echoed, gripping the wheel a little more tightly. Malcolm's neighborhood was right by there, God dammit.

The drive took five hours thanks to rush hour trapping me on the beltway, and it was nearing dusk by the time I finally pulled into my brother's driveway. There were several cars parked along the curb but only one in the driveway, and the only car I recognized—my sister's white SUV.

Behind the house was a forest full of pine trees, their dark silhouettes like jagged teeth biting into the rump of the setting sun. I felt my skin crawl as I watched them sway gently. How could he live so close to so many of them?

"Hey, Jason!" my sister said, greeting me at the door. She smiled and pulled me into a bear hug. She smelled of coco butter and mint.

"Jason!" Malcolm yelled from the living room. He was sitting on the couch with some of his friends whose names I didn't remember and would quickly forget again after he reminded me. He waved me over to join them in watching the game. There was a big window in the living room that lead to a patio.

"You're really not scared, are you?" I asked, sitting in a chair across from the couch.

Malcolm followed my gaze out the patio door towards the forest beyond. The pines were still swaying in the breeze. "Oh, you mean the trees? I heard about that Deer Grove shit, but nah, man, don't worry about it. They leave me well enough alone. It's not like its every tree, you know what I mean."

"It only takes one…"

Malcolm tilted his chin over to the corner of the room. Propped up against the wall was a black and yellow chainsaw. "Luxury model, leather grip and everything."

I wasn't convinced. But before I could speak more about it, Jason and his friends diverted their attention back to the game, cheering and cursing. A goal was scored, apparently.

I went to the kitchen. Carla was cooking. Gumbo, string beans, candied yams, and a bunch of other things. The ice cream cake was in the freezer. Oreo flavor, of course. Malcolm's favorite. Mine too, if I was being honest. I offered to help with the cooking, but she was almost done. So, I settled for setting the table.

"Didn't think you'd show, honestly," Carla said, carrying a crockpot full of gumbo into the dining room and setting it on the table. "Given how you never leave the city and all."

I shrugged, putting a fork beside a plate. It was possibly a salad fork, but I could never tell the difference. "It means a lot to you."

Carla chuckled. "But it's Malcolm's birthday."

I gestured to all the food and decorations. "Doesn't change what I said."

Carla looked around at the amazing job she'd done. "I guess I do take family parties a little too seriously..." She nodded approvingly of her handiwork. "Well, time to eat!"

We ate and drank, and perhaps I drank a little too much. But unlike my brother, I was able to find the couch before passing out. The next morning, it was just me, Malcolm and Carla, and Malcolm was still passed out on the floor.

When Carla started working on tidying up the house, I felt obliged to help. It was the least I could do after missing helping with dinner. Halfway through sweeping the confetti and streamers off the ground, I nudged Malcom who was still snoring on the floor. Asshole. We'd be done faster if he helped us clean his own goddamn house, but Carla just told me to leave him be.

"But it's not his birthday anymore," I argued. "You gotta quit babying him."

"It's fine, Jason. We'll be done soon."

But not soon enough. It felt like the afternoon had snuck up on us, and I was getting worried about being caught on the road after dark outside the city. Carla tried to calm me down, but I wasn't having it. Maybe it was the wind, but I'd spied one of the trees moving outside the patio an hour ago.

"You should get going, too," I said to Carla as I headed for the door. "Just leave the rest Malcolm already. He can wash his own dishes."

"I'll be finished in thirty," she said, sticking her head out of the kitchen doorway. "Just gotta finish scrubbing the crockpot. But you go ahead. I'll see you for Thanksgiving? I think I'm gonna try to fry a turkey this year."

"Sounds good," I sighed, not knowing what else to say. "Later."

I headed out and briskly walked to my car. In the corner of my vision, I could see the pines swaying. But then I stopped. There wasn't any breeze. I looked at the sky. The clouds weren't even moving. I jumped in my car and drove off. The whole drive home I kept looking in my rearview mirror. Trees couldn't keep up with a car. I had to relax—keep my eyes on the road before I crashed into something. But I couldn't shake the feeling the fucking tree was after me. When I got home I flipped open my laptop out of habit, and then I saw it. A news article with a headline as bold as baseball bat to the mouth.

Suspected Tree Attack in West Creek: *A car was found overturned on a side road in West Creek. There was one victim found at the scene. A 29 year-old woman by the name of Carla Matthews. Given the amount of pine needles left at the scene, police suspect this was a tree attack, making it the third one this month in the state.*

I closed my laptop and leaned back on the couch. The shock was overwhelming to the point of making me numb. Though I could only imagine what I'd feel like in a few minutes. But one thing I knew for sure, clearly now, like a polished ax head, was that I hated trees. Fucking hated all of them.

Hecksin & the Real Witch

By Phillip Hamilton

□□□

THE moment Hecksin sat across from me at the small patio table just outside of the *Heart-Attack Caffeine Bar*, the sun vanished behind a set of gray clouds, exasperating his custom black Gucci robe and sun hat, drawing a heavy shadow across his pale, vampiric face, covered largely by a pair of oversized designer sunglasses. It wasn't supposed to rain that day; maybe it wouldn't. I couldn't help feeling, though, after we shook hands and he took off his sunglasses and set them between us on the table, revealing a wide set of unnatural yellow eyes, that he had stolen the sunlight.

If you don't know Hecksin, you're not paying enough attention. The twenty-something-year-old Ohio native is often regarded as one of the most important figures in the growing niche of "witch-hop" artists. His dark, occult-laden bars, rapped (and just as often sung) in a droning demeanor over grimy, eardistressing beats filled with wailing guitars and buzzing keys quickly skyrocketed the artist to underground fame over the past two years, paving the way for a "gothic revival" of sorts in high schools across the country. Everybody wants to be him, and if they don't want to be him, they want to be with him, and if they don't want either of those things, they're probably an angry, religious parent who gets off on outrage.

"Last year all these Christian evangelical Nazi parents got on me for getting naked and nailing a dead goat to a cross live on stage," he tells me, gazing deeply into the foam on his latte, "but it's like, okay. What do you want me to do about it? These same parents used to watch Ozzy Osbourne bite the heads off bats every night and flash their tits for Motley Crue. What separates a bat from a goat? If you don't want your kids at my show don't let them go to my show. Good luck with that, but it is what it is."

When he talks, it's hard to look at anything but his teeth. While Hecksin's style is mostly based around witches, he's also taken the liberty to shave a few of his teeth into sharp, vampire-like fangs. When I ask him why he did that, he shrugs, picking at the scone in front of him with his long, equally sharp nails. I can't quite tell if they're real or not.

"It's just cool, I guess," he tells me. "It makes the parents mad. Once I saw what sort of power I had against these uptight pricks, and what sort of influence I had on young people who vibe with dark shit, I kind of just leaned into it. I started blasting Christianity a lot more during my shows, started doing more on-stage rituals with pentagrams and goats and cats and all that. The crucifixion was just art – it was just an idea that came to me one night and I knew I had to do it. It's fun, you know, to see the contrast between the positive feedback from the fans and the negative feedback from Christian fascist assholes. It's all just so silly. They don't seem to get that all they're doing is lifting me out of the underground and exposing me to more people than I ever thought possible. I feed off their outrage – I'm a vampire for that shit."

It's about twenty minutes into our conversation when a young Hecksin fan comes up off the street to get a photo with his hero. The kid looks like any other hype-beast out there; Yeezy's on his feet, Supreme on his chest, Bape on his shorts and a ratty Yankees hat to top it all off. He must be 13 at most; as Hecksin tells me, his fanbase tends to be between 13 and 27 years old.

He tells me that a year ago this would never happen. People only started to recognize him publicly after his song *W1cA* went viral on TikTok, inspiring a controversial trend where kids make it appear as if they're sacrificing their family cat in their bedroom closet. When I ask him about the trend – the 13-year-old hype-beast long gone – the mood shifts. Hecksin gets quiet and finally takes a bite of his picked-apart scone. He shakes his head; he puts his sunglasses back on and adjusts his robe. Then, he sighs, and for the first time, he drops the character.

"The cat trend, you know, I thought it was cool when it was happening, but it kind of gives me bad vibes now," he tells me. "The trend was all fake for the most part, but I remember reading about this one kid who, like, actually killed his cat for the trend – I'm sure you heard about that – and when I read that I kind of wondered for a second if things went too far. If I was playing into this character too much. When I 'sacrifice cats' on stage, I mean… maybe this breaks the illusion, I've never told anyone this before, but it's all fake. Same with the goat. It's just art. I've never actually killed an animal on stage; I think if I did that I'd never book another venue again in my life. I keep doing it, though, even after that because it's what the people want. It's the hole I've dug myself into. I can't blame myself for what one stupid kid did and I can't turn back time. Besides, I… you know, I've never told anyone this either, but I absolutely paid the price for that kid's sin. I paid the price big-time."

The barista comes over and we both order another drink; Hecksin, an Americano that's almost as black as his robe, and another latte for me. She takes our empty dishes from the table and eyes Hecksin. It's impossible to tell whether she recognizes him and hates him, recognizes him and is too shy to ask for an autograph or just wants this "freak" out of her "caffeine bar." When she's finally gone, I press him on the story.

"What do you mean by 'paid the price?'" I ask. Somehow, the sky seems to get darker and the volume of the city behind us seems to get lower, as if setting the mood.

"I'll tell you," he says. "I swore I'd never tell anyone, but I think it's time. I haven't stopped thinking about it since it happened, if we're being honest, and there's something about you that… I trust you. Just promise me you'll publish it. Publish the whole story no matter how bad it makes me look, and it's going to make me look bad. Understand?"

I nod, adjusting the recorded on the table and flipping to a blank page in my notebook.

"I'm ready," I say. Then, he tells me.

□ □ □

IT was a sold-out show; the crowd was electric. Thousands of sweaty teens and young adults moshed and swayed and screamed at the top of their lungs as Hecksin rattled through his growing discography of hits. A single photograph of the crowd would be enough to give the average parent a heart attack. Most of the kids were dressed in black, and not just black t-shirts and jeans, but robes and thigh-high boots and gloves and hoods, like they were part of a cult. Many of them cross-dressed. They wore gray facepaint with blood-red accents on their lips and under their eyes. All the girls were dressed in fishnet stockings, showing as much skin as possible while keeping to the gothic theme of cut-apart robes that accentuated their cleavage. Hundreds of attendees were tripping on molly and LSD and mushrooms. Some of them even wore these big, pointy witch hats that Hecksin had started selling at his shows – they were his number one selling merch item. The vibes that night were exactly what not only Hecksin, but any artist for that matter, dreamed of, and the way the crowd cheered and screamed as he "sacrificed the cat" that night filled him with energy.

After the sacrifice, just before he broke into *W1cCA*, Hecksin called out to the crowd, the cat's fake blood all over his robes, "How many real witches we got in here tonight?" The entire crowd erupted in cheers, caring very little if they were real witches or not. Hecksin repeated the question and the crowd erupted again, all except for one girl in the front row with green lipstick that matched her hypnotic eyes, her face covered in piercings. The two made eye-contact and held it, Hecksin falling quiet for a few moments as the crowd hollered and the guitarist played the opening riff of *W1cCA*. He wanted her. No, he needed her, and he decided, right then and there, that she would be his.

□□□

AFTER the show, Hecksin sat at the merch table for a while, signing merchandise and listening to every kid at the show's sob story about how his music saved their life and how he allowed them to be who they wanted to be and blah, blah, blah. He appreciated it – really, he did – but there was only so much he could take at this point in his career. He was ready to move past the era where he had to sit at merch tables and sign shit and listen to the same story over and over again. Thankfully, that era was coming fast.

This would be his last show in the city for a while, and in a few days he'd be on the road with his bandmates on their first headlining tour around the country. The only thing Hecksin was going to miss about the merch table was the girls. Every other girl who came up to him, whether she was of age or not, gave him a phone number or an Instagram handle or invited him to a party or to their apartment for what would obviously turn into a hookup. For the first time in his life, Hecksin had options; he'd quickly gone from a skinny nerd that nobody wanted to touch to one of the most desirable, sickly white men on earth and it made him feel powerful. Some nights, Hecksin wondered if he truly had made a deal with the devil. Maybe, one night on-stage, he'd accidentally managed to make some pact with Satan or some other dark force while drawing the pentagram and chanting his phony Satanic chant over the fake, blood-filled cat or the nailed-to-a-cross goat. He always quickly dismissed that thought, though. Hecksin knew it was all bullshit. He knew that it was hypocritical and nonsensical to believe in witchcraft or Satan when he was so dead-set against believing in Christ. There can't be one without the other, as he saw it. Sometimes he wondered if his fans realized that, too. Not that he would ever tell them.

That night at the merch table, Hecksin ended up with a thick stack of numbers and usernames, but he burned them all from his roster of potential hookups when, finally, the girl with the green lipstick showed up. There was something about her that stood out to Hecksin in the crowd of similarly-styled women. She fit the bill more than the others, but he couldn't quite decide why. He signed a copy of his CD for her and started making small talk, eagerly waiting for her to give him something else – a number or a name or an address, anything – but it wasn't happening. Then, she asked him a question.

"Are you a real witch?"

The question brought a smile to his face. He tapped his marker against the table and looked her up and down, blood rushing downward as he struggled not to look at her breasts. He'd thought about the question a few times before, but the only real answer was "no." Hecksin was just a character. It was an amalgamation of his teenage fascination with the occult and horror movies and Marilyn Manson brought to life in a profitable way. Hecksin had learned a little bit about the occult over the years, especially since taking on the character full-time for the benefit of his art, but he was an amateur at best. He couldn't tell you the different denominations of witchcraft, or what a Wiccan really was, or how to perform any given ritual. He mainly just liked the aesthetic. He was a poser. But, that night at the merch table, Hecksin was in character. He was playing his role, and who was he to break the illusion?

"Of course," he said, now scratching the surface of the table with his pen. "Are you?"

"Would you like to find out?" she asked, licking her lips. He felt nervous all of a sudden, like he was back in high school, a skinny geek posing as an angsty emo, watching his English class crush from the back row knowing he didn't have a chance in hell. Only, he did have a chance, now. Hecksin nodded and pulled his phone from his pocket, opened his "Contacts" app and slid it towards her.

"No," she said, sliding it back. "Tonight. Let's go somewhere. I think you're free right now, right?"

Hecksin leaned to the right and looked behind the green-lipped girl. There was nobody else in line. The venue had almost entirely cleared out, even though he could have sworn the line was longer just a moment ago. Had he really spent that much time talking with her that everyone else just left? It felts as though he'd only said a handful of words. Whatever the case, Hecksin didn't linger on it too long. Instead, he got up, brought her to the backroom, told his band that he was going home, then left with the real witch. A moment later he received a text message from his drummer. "Have fun, asshole ;)" it read. He planned on it.

□ □ □

HER name was Shelter; at least, that's what she told him as the two "witches" walked towards his apartment in the dead of night, guided by the pull of the moon. They didn't say much as they made their way through the empty streets, Hecksin only speaking up after looking behind him to see a stray cat, its black coat reflecting the light of passing cars. It was following them.

"You know this guy?" he asked, teasingly. Shelter stopped in her tracks, leaned down and extended a limp hand forward, running her fingers through the cat's thin hair.

"Yes, actually. He's been following me for a few days now," she said. "I can't quite figure out what he wants, though. What his purpose is." The cat looked up at Hecksin and meowed, moving toward him to rub itself against his boots. Hecksin leaned down and pet the cat, scratching its small chin. "Do you own a cat?" Shelter asked, standing up straight.

"No, I don't," he said. "I'm too busy with shows, especially now that we're going on tour. I guess we could use a tour cat, though." Shelter thought for a moment, then shook her head.

"No, I don't think that's his destiny," she said, "but if you don't mind, I'd like to take him upstairs with us. It's supposed to rain and I'd like to keep him dry." There wasn't a single moment where Hecksin thought about refusing her request. The more he looked at her, the more he wanted her, and he wasn't prepared to do anything to mess that up. So, Shelter picked up the small black cat and held it in her arms as he unlocked the front door of the building and ushered her into the elevator and down the hall to his apartment, where, in moments, the two would be engaging in Hecksin's favorite kind of magic.

□□□

"INTERESTING décor," Shelter said, placing the cat down on Hecksin's hardwood floor. His place looked like it was taken straight from an Ikea catalogue; it smelled like a fancy candle. The furniture was practical and boring, the television was too big, and the paintings that hung on the wall were basic, comprising mostly of cityscapes by nameless artists and abstract pieces that looked like they were painted by high school art students. Nothing except for the occasional framed horror movie poster screamed "occult," which became increasingly apparent after he turned the lights on.

"It's nothing special, I know," Hecksin said, "but it's temporary. I've been broke all my life until recently. After this tour I'm hoping to upgrade."

He walked into the kitchen, stood in front of the sink and washed as much makeup off his face as he could, doing an overall crummy job of it. Then, he pulled out a bottle of Jack Daniels and a few glasses and poured a little into one. "Would you like a drink?" he asked, but she shook her head.

"I don't drink," she said. "I wouldn't want to dull myself. But don't let me stop you." She made her way all around the small apartment, running her hand over the couch, the loveseat, the doorknobs, feeling everything she could. The cat did the same, leaving its black hair on every surface that wasn't hard and cold. Hecksin watched her the entire time, unable to take his eyes off her except to drink. One the drink was done, he became overwhelmed with lust. He had to have her now; the way she looked at him, he knew she wanted the same.

Hecksin made his move; he walked over to Shelter, standing in front of the couch, and grabbed her waist, kissing her deeply. She kissed him back, running her cold hands up and down his body and pulling off his jacket, then pulling off his shirt. A swathe of his remaining face-paint came off with it, exposing the man behind the paint, and she grinned as she turned him around and he sat on the couch and she straddled his lap. He pulled away for a moment.

"Do you want me to take the rest of the makeup off?" he asked, panting, "It's kind of itchy."

"Do you want to take it off?" she asked, taking off her top.

"Nah, I'm good," he said. She pushed back to his face and kept on kissing him, rubbing his chest as he moved his hands up her body and grabbed her breasts, pulling off her bra and tossing it to the ground. A few moments later, she pulled back again and reached into her pocket, pulling out a small vial of pink liquid.

"Drink this," she said, "and then we can fuck." Hecksin stared at the bottle, corked and without a label, with little bubbles floating in it like hand sanitizer.

"You're not trying to roofie me, are you?" he asked, half-jokingly. She popped the cork off and took a small drink herself as if to prove it was safe, then stuck out her tongue, showing a faint pink streak. She handed Hecksin the bottle. He shot back the liquid, eager to get back to the action.

Minutes passed. The witches fondled and caressed and kiss, Shelter dry-grinding on top of him, still in a sitting position, teasing him, never quite giving him exactly what he wanted. At some point, Hecksin looked to his left and saw the cat sitting on the arm of the couch, watching them with a blank look. When he looked back up, Shelter was gone. She wasn't on top of him anymore; she was nowhere to be seen, somehow gone within the blink of an eye. He called her name once, twice, then tried to stand up. He couldn't. His muscles were stiff and heavy as if weighed down by some invisible force. He shouted again, violently, trying his hardest to move with no luck. The cat stared. Then, from the kitchen, came Shelter, wearing nothing but the robe Hecksin performed in that night.

"You're nothing but a poser," she said, walking closer to the sweating artist. "You think this life is a joke, don't you? Just a way to get pussy. Is that correct?" Hecksin was in full panic mode now. He shouted once for help, then tried again and found his voice had grown hoarse. He couldn't speak; his tongue and his lips were numb, just as heavy as his limbs. *It was a roofie,* he thought, *it had to be some kind of roofie.* All Hecksin could do was sweat as a million non-descript thoughts and regrets raced through his head. Then he noticed the chalk in her hand.

Shelter pushed the coffee table to the side of the room, the rug underneath dragging along under it. She leaned down, chanting something under her breath as she drew a big circle on the ground. Hecksin wasn't a real witch, but he knew what a pentagram looked like.

"You didn't believe me when I said I was a real witch, did you?" She asked. "How many girls have come back here after saying they were real witches? How many have come back here even without that claim? You're no different than the next rockstar asshole, no matter how much makeup you put on. You sing these vulnerable, dark songs that strike a chord with so many young, vulnerable people and then you take advantage of that for your own sexual gratification, all while making a mockery of witchcraft. As long as she's willing, nothing else matters, right? Do I have you figured out?"

Shelter stood in the middle of the complete pentagram, barefoot, and took a few delicate steps towards Hecksin. The cat came to her side, rubbing up against her legs. She reached down to her pants, still in a pile by the bed, and fished around in the pocket, retrieving her knife. Hecksin was sure he was about to die. She walked back over to his still-petrified body, straddled him like before, and held the blade against his chest. He was ashamed to find himself a little bit turned on amidst the panic, not that his body would let him act on it. That feeling quickly left when she pulled the blade across his pectorals, eliciting a thin stream of blood that carried itself down his body.

Shelter put her lips to the wound and sucked. She picked up the small vial once containing the pink potion and spit his blood inside. Then, she walked over to the pentagram and poured the blood right into the center of it. Hecksin's vision blurred; the room seemed to quake for a moment as Shelter began to chant. As she chanted, a black tower of smoke lifted up from the center of the pentagram – from the splash of his blood – and moved like a snake toward Hecksin, shelter never ceasing her chant as she and the cat watched it with careful eyes. The smoke split into two streams; one slithered into Hecksin's nostrils and the other into the cat's. Neither of them moved a muscle.

Finally, the room seemed to brighten. The air got lighter as Shelter walked back over to Hecksin once more. She ran her finger across his still bleeding wound and licked some of the blood, wanting another taste.

"The potion will wear off soon enough," she said, stripping off his robe and collecting her clothes. "Tomorrow, your bandmates will fall ill. In the next few days, so will you. Your tour bus will cease to function and so will your voice. All the venues you have booked will cancel your shows. Everything that could go wrong for a touring performer, will go wrong, and the only way you can remedy it is to sacrifice this very cat on the pentagram in front of you. I'll leave instructions on the kitchen table. It's up to you whether you fulfill the task or not. I sincerely hope you don't, but I have a strong feeling you will."

Before she left, she leaned back toward Hecksin's face one final time and kissed his unmoving lips. She put her clothes back on, grabbed her things, said, "Goodbye, William," and left the apartment without another word. The cat rubbed up against his stiff legs, purring, then jumped into his lap and curled up into a ball. She fell asleep immediately. Hecksin stayed up, stun-locked to the couch the rest of the night, his mind wrestling with itself, trying to comprehend what just happened.

⬜ ⬜ ⬜

THE next morning, just as the green lipped witch had promised, the drummer called Hecksin. The rented tour bus needed to go to the mechanic's shop and the keyboard player caught some kind of flu. The drummer didn't feel too hot, either, and the guitarist had spent the whole morning puking up his guts. When Hecksin tried to respond, to beg his bandmates to get rest and power through and find a new bus, his voice was raspy and weak. It was as if there was a clamp on his throat; the words could hardly make it off his tongue and he was winded after only a short attempt at speaking. The drummer knew the tour wasn't going to happen; so did Hecksin.

"I was so frustrated I threw my phone at the wall," he tells me, his coffee now ice cold in the gray afternoon shade. "I never called the police, either. What was I going to say? What kind of a cop would believe that some witch – some real witch – came into my home, roofied, and put a curse on me? They probably would've thought it was just another publicity stunt. I didn't even have any real evidence she'd been there except the instructions she left on my table, and once I read them, I swear to God this is true, the text disappeared. Vanished. Poof. Gone, just like that."

"Did you ever see her again?" I asked. He shook his head.

"I never saw her again. I doubt her real name was even Shelter. I tried searching for a while, but I've given up at this point. What would I even do if I ran into her? What's the point? I think I'd be too scared to go near her."

"Do you believe that she's a real witch?"

He picked up the coffee and swirled it around, gazing into it

91

deeply as if considering taking a drink.

"I know she's a real witch," he said. "And I know I'm not. I never have been a real witch and I've never wanted to be a real witch. I'm just an artist – a provocateur, I guess, and that's all I ever will be. I might not even be that once this interview comes out and everyone sees how much of a phony and a scumbag I am. But I deserve it. I didn't expect for this interview to go this way, for me to tell you all this, but I needed to, and I'm ready for whatever comes my way because of it. I'm just a poser. I'm a man playing a character that's been played a million times before, and I'm going to keep playing that character. I guess I just want people, all those impressionable kids and those uptight Christian pricks, to know that their actions have consequences. That maybe they shouldn't shape their lives around their idols and be something they're not just to fit in with a crowd. The majority of the people at my shows are posers just like me and that's okay. But they need to realize that and know that there are dark things at play on this earth. You can only benefit from being a poser for so long before reality – or surreality – comes and slaps you in the face. In my case, it roofied me, sliced my chest and put a curse on me. I don't wish that shit on anyone, human or cat."

🞏🞏🞏

THERE was no good way to continue the interview after a story like that, so Hecksin and I shook hands and left the caffeine bar together. It never rained that day. The clouds parted as we paid our bills and left through the front entrance to wait for our Ubers. I ran the story through my head on repeat, thinking about the media storm it might spark, the reactions it would garner, the places it might take me. I almost felt bad knowing that I had to, had to publish it. Hecksin pulled out a cigarette and puffed away. I don't smoke, but when he offered me one I took it, lighting it off of his like they do in the movies. Then, I asked him one last question.

"This is off the record," I said as we stood against the caffeine bar's brick wall, "but I have to ask… you just came off a successful world tour. You just put out your new album, you have an appearance at the Grammy's coming up and you have a new song going viral on TikTok." I knew the answer, but I asked the question anyways: "Did you kill the cat?"

He pulled the cigarette from his mouth and blew a plume of white smoke into the air, then coughed into his fist and spit up some tar. A black Uber pulled up to the curb; I wasn't sure if it was mine or his.

"I prefer the term 'sacrifice,'" he said, dropping the butt to the pavement, stomping it out, then stepping towards the car, "and that's on the record." He pulled the rear-passenger-side door open, climbed into the car, closed it, and the car sped down the road. For a brief moment, I could have sworn I saw the waitress who'd just served our coffee standing on the opposite side of the street wearing green lipstick. I blinked and she was gone.

□□□

Portraits of St. Kevin's

By Shan

FROM a swampy bank of a certain river in an ancient little city in Ireland's south, one can look across the water and up along the hills on the far shore, thick and green with seething life, and there have one's gaze met by the dark, empty stare of a dead thing; from a dozen eyes of scorched brick and shattered glass, the burnt-out carcass of St Kevin's looks out over the city below. An old asylum, with a history steeped in the sort of pain and squalor peculiar to such asylums – and to Irish asylums perhaps more so than others – one could be forgiven, even in this day and age, for imagining the place to be haunted. One cannot help but stare at this mass of wooden flesh and red-brick bone, the way one's eyes cling to a roadkill-rabbit in a ditch or a dead dog washed up on the bank of a river, bloated with water and decay. One also can't but help feel as though something is staring back, as though one has locked eyes with something old and living and mysterious. We may be tempted to wonder what dreams and memories echo through those charred and corrupted hallways. And yet, whatever about its own ghosts, it is the place itself that is truly haunting, and each evening, as the sun descends into the west behind St Kevin's, all of Cork city is submerged in the long shadow of madness.

What is this uncanny presence watching us from the far hill? Which words must we use, which lines must we sketch, to give shape to the formless and capture the essence of the place? A mere factual description won't suffice; this place has a character, just as much as any creature of flesh and blood. How might we characterise St Kevin's?

The answer is enticingly intuitive: we characterize it the same way we might characterise a man or woman, and recreate some aspect of their essence in ink or watercolor paints or pencil lead. We tell stories; we sketch portraits. But the tale is in the telling, of course, and the portrait is in the painting. We might tell any number of stories about a man, or have any number of artists paint his portrait, and each of these replications would be unique. Each would have their own subtleties of style and character. Our impressions of our subject might vary greatly depending on the stories we tell about him.

So, too, with St. Kevin's; the spirit of a building is a nebulous thing, much like the nameless presence we may feel watching us from the void in the sockets of a human skull. All houses may have spirits, in either sense of the word, but it is we who give them stories and histories and names – it is we who shape them into ghosts.

So what, then, does St Kevin's see, perched high in its lofty, lonely nest? Does it grin over sordid scenes in smoky back-rooms, a decades-long fever dream of anxious eyes set deep into hooded sockets; of stale foam, yellowed like pus on pints of thick, dark intoxicants, clinging to the lips of sloppy, slapping mouths – mouths possessed by spirits of an altogether different kind; a nightly nightmare of sweat and smoke and booze? How many young men, how much young flesh, has it seen beaten and bled? How many has it seen killed? How many holy virgins, vestal and unvested, has it seen despoiled at Dionysus' altar, sacrifices to that horned god who captured madness in a bottle – then later put it on tap?

Or perhaps a note of tragedy. How many young lovers have honeyed and romanced beneath the silent stare of those fire-scarred old bricks? How many of those same lovers have they seen betrayed, jilted and heartbroken? We might imagine a scene by moonlight of a young woman, leaning over the edge of a high bridge and staring into the churning, inky black below. Perhaps she looks up, and perhaps she fancies that the moonlight gleams on the broken panes of St Kevin's' windows much as it must be gleaming on her own brimming tears. We might feel the old husk of a place straining in distress, urging itself to help; it has seen enough death, and more suffering than any living mind could bear. We might feel it struggling to set its rotted planks and rusted pipes into some sort of motion, to find some semblance of a voice with which to cry out, "*Stop!* Think of the coming dawn," but to no avail. The old asylum has no voice with which to sob, and none shall hear it mourn yet another whom it failed to save.

And what of that coming dawn? How does the warmth of sunrise feel on those walls? Is it a joy? Now that it is abandoned, now that the screaming and suffering are ended, can even a place such as this bask in the summer sun? Might it even take some pride to stand aloft over the little city, a testament to our sins, and a warning for our future? One could certainly imagine that, after all this time in silence, the place feels a certain liberation. No more pain; no more sickness. Old ghosts still stalk the winding corridors of its memory, but the streets below are rich with colour and filled with free, living people; in the morning light, the city begins to sing their joys and sorrows. Even after long decades housing fear and pain, viewed in this light and from this angle, one could certainly imagine St Kevin's to be optimistic – perhaps one could even imagine it happy.

Perhaps; perhaps not. Perhaps instead, St Kevin's snarls and hisses and spits at the rising sun, "How dare you cast your rays upon this place? How dare the sun shine here, on these halls, where guilty and innocent alike festered, where sickness howled alone in the darkness?" Perhaps songs of the city below ring harsh and dissonant like a cruel song of schoolyard mockery. Perhaps the dawn's rays burn like blasphemy. Would we dare to even whisper the word "happiness" in a place such as this? The same place, but different portraits – you get the picture.

One more illustration, just for good measure – let's take the rats. Old buildings are full of the things, squirming and chittering and breeding in the dark. There's not many pleasant things that one can say about rats – not about wild rats, at least. But what of the unpleasant things we might say? How might these rodents color the character of our red-brick ruin? One example might focus on the vermin themselves, scurrying through the pipes and between the blackened timbers like maggots wriggling through the rancid flesh of a dying animal. The asylum here takes on the character of a great beast, gutted and broken on the hillside. Its soul is dumb, wailing soundlessly with the silenced voices of those who had wailed within its walls, and still the rats burrow deeper, *deeper* into its diseased flesh. This is a house of pain and sickness.

Another little tale might see a boy of thirteen dare to plumb the asylum's depths, a modern Theseus braving his labyrinth. We might imagine a schoolyard dare, a girl to impress, a jeering gang of juveniles egging him on – in any case, he climbs the steep hill towards the building and tells himself that he is not afraid. St Kevin's looms ever taller the closer he draws, the windows studying him, stern and unblinking. Our hero feels the sweat dampen his shirtsleeves and sting his underarms. He is beginning to lose heart. It is as he moves to climb through a ground-floor window that our young Theseus meets his minotaur; a great black rat, as big as a tomcat and chirping like a demented songbird, darts across the window-frame, mere inches from the young boy's face. The wetness isn't just under his arms anymore, and it might bring us no end of delight to see *ár ghile mear* bolting down the hill and screeching like a toddler. Yet comical as the scene may be, years later, when he recounts his tale to his psychoanalyst, she notes, perhaps struggling to contain her own laughter, that it is not the rat that haunts him, but the stern judgement he had read on the facade of the building itself. Here, unlike before, St Kevin's found a voice in the form of a fat black rat, and with that voice it spoke the words, "this is no place for children".

Perhaps my own favourite of the countless stories we might tell about the rats of St Kevin's sees an old man huddled in rags amidst the building's shattered old bones. His father had told him, when he was young, that if he didn't straighten himself out, he would end up in St Kevin's; the asylum had long since closed down, and two years had passed since the fire tore through the building, but time had proved his father right. His father had *always* been right, about everything. Tonight, the old man dies with a needle in his arm, and the last face he sees is that of bloated rat watching him from the far corner of what is left of the room. He does not hear the building grieve. He does not know how St Kevin's wishes it could take him in his arms and bear him to paradise. He does not know that he dies in the presence of a friend who loves him more dearly than it has ever loved anyone – and why should it not? They are alike. This man came into the world screaming and formless in the full, unbridled potential of a newborn life. He had not asked for what he was given; these rooms had not asked to serve as prisons for the sick, and these windows had not asked to ring with cries of fear and anguish. And now the two of them, the old man and the building that cradles him in his death, will meet the same end, abandoned and decrepit; they will be food for the rats.

Through all of these tellings and tales, however, the place is still recognizably itself; a different portrait, perhaps even different painters, but nonetheless the subject shines forth. Through all the endless variety of form and feeling we might ascribe to St Kevin's, the madness and misery, triumph and tragedy, it remains, a solitary monolith meeting our gaze from across the river. The scenes and stories may, as with any more *tangible* character, help us to view the old ruin through a different lens, as it were, or to see it in a different light. The soul of the place, however, simply broods, impervious to definition, try as we might to capture it within the pages of a notebook or on the surface of a canvas. We may be tempted, as noted before, to let ourselves sink into comfortable, familiar fantasies of pale spectres with names and faces roaming those blackened halls in the night, yearning to right some oh-so human wrong; but such an image fails to capture the true nature of the place, the unitary, indefinable essence that echoes through those hallways and permeates those walls. We may fail to grasp that what watches us from those window frames as we stand on our swampy bank is utterly and irreconcilably *other*, regardless of the stories we may tell about it. As we have said, places like this are not haunted – they haunt us, and no matter where we tread along the banks of the Lee, we may still from time to time feel the hairs on our necks bristle in the gaze of the dead thing we have named St Kevin's.

The Sub

by Orlik Zarion

THE night before I moved out of my brother's apartment I told him to tell me a three cigarette story and he didn't disappoint. We took our seats on the balcony and he got right into it.

"You remember that guy who lived with me before you left Bainbridge?" he asked.

"Yeah. The firefighter," I said, getting ready to light. "Doug something?"

My brother nodded.

"Do you remember anything specific about him?" he asked.

"Well," I said. "He had greasy hair, I remember that. I only met him like twice though. Didn't he drive a 2002?"

"He did," said my brother. "Which—funny story by the way—he actually wrecked it two months ago going over the pass. He almost died, but that's neither here nor there. Did you happen to remember what religion he was?"

"Christian?" I guessed.

"Specifically though."

"Catholic?"

"Exactly right," he said, sitting back in his chair. "Now that's not exactly important to the events of the story I'm about to tell you, but just think about all the things you tend to associate with Catholics. I feel like it adds something, knowing Doug was a Papist."

"I trust you," I said, matching his relaxed posture.

"Well alright," he said. "You remember Doug, but you probably don't remember his girlfriend, do you? Her name was December, and yeah, I know it sounds made up, but I swear that was her name. December Vernon. She was one hundred percent exactly what the name suggests. Classic beauty, but with something weird in there. Pale. Blonde with green eyes, and skinny too. Pure death. She dressed like she was the total opposite though, which is a common issue these days. It's like, I know somewhere in there there's a perfectly hot skeleton hiding under layers of baggy clothing."

"I get the picture." I said. "She was attractive, but dressed for an ugly era."

"Right, and so when I met her I was surprised because Doug wasn't exactly like… I mean Doug was like… you know? He was a slob, you know? Like me. So I pulled him aside and asked him: no offense, but how is this even possible? You know what he said?"

"Lay it on me."

He tapped off a bit of ash.

"He said she liked the way he choked her."

"That was his reason?" I said.

"That was *her* reason," said my brother. "And I know what you're thinking. Beautiful girl, who wouldn't choke her? That's what I said to Doug, but he set me straight. He told me she told him, it's not just putting your hand around her neck and squeezing. It's an exchange of energy that can't be faked. There are hands that are made for choking, and hands that aren't. Apparently Doug has the first kind of hands, and she'd been trying to find a pair like that for a long time."

"Sweet deal," I said. "But I don't see where this is going."

"Okay I'll speed up a bit," he said. "She was a crazy person. She got into some drama with her roommates over this hemlock patch in their backyard. They wanted the landlord to pull it all out, but he never got around to it. December wanted the hemlock to stay, but the roommates didn't care. It's poison, they said. It's got to go. So one day, the roommates got together while she was at work and they just pulled out all the hemlock. She exploded when she found out. Like, I still don't understand why it meant that much to her, but she tore apart the house. Screaming at the roommates and breaking stuff. It was actually bad. Doug had to pull her out of there before she killed somebody, and knowing what I found out about her later, I legitimately think… I don't know."

"What did you find out?"

"Just listen. That's what I'm telling you, but you have to let me to tell it correctly. I'm developing a case against her."

I figured at the rate I was smoking, I'd probably be done with three cigs before he was halfway through his story, so I held up for a minute just listening. "Proceed," I said.

"Alright, Doug came to me and asked if December could stay here for a while. I said yes, which I think is a pretty kind thing to do seeing as I could have said no. Only she wasn't grateful at all. When she showed up she threw all her stuff in the living room and didn't say anything. I kept trying to start a conversation with her but she only gave me these weird inadequate responses. I gave Doug a look like, bro your girl sucks, and he made a face like he was sorry. Then I heard them arguing in your room."

"The door," I said. My brother's apartment was old and the doorway to my room was slightly warped in a way that prevented total closure. Anything that happened in that room was easily heard from the kitchen, where my brother ate his meals staring out the window.

"That's right," he said. "I heard everything they did, but before you start thinking you know where I'm going with this, just hold on. Yes. I heard them having sex, but that's actually where this gets weird. They weren't at all quiet about it. All the time, I'd hear them from the hallway when I got home from work. And one day I heard them going at it, but then I remembered: hang on, Doug's in Idaho on a fire."

"She was cheating on him," I said.

"That's what I thought. I couldn't tell Doug because he didn't have service. Then the next night I heard the same thing. Two people moaning. She was in there with a guy, only this time it was like 3am, so I made up my mind I'd knock on the door and sort of act like I was just trying to get them to quiet down, but purposefully knock too hard so the door would swing open. When I got up to the door I heard the guy's voice real low, saying some pretty reprehensible shit. She started to get loud again, so I knocked hard and the door swung open. She was laying there in just a t-shirt with her hair all messed up and her eyes in the back of her head. I said I knew she was cheating on Doug, and I walked into the room thinking the guy rolled under the bed or something. She stood up and started screaming at me, and I looked under the bed but the guy wasn't there. There was nowhere to hide and no way he could have gotten out that fast. I looked back at her, and that's when it hit me. She was not an ordinary person. She was a fucking creep."

"There was nobody else?" I said.

"Nobody else. She must have been doing both voices."

"Well that's a pretty embarrassing kink," I said, "But I get the feeling you didn't build all this up just to tell me you heard a girl talking to herself."

"You're exactly right. It gets weirder, but you've finished ciggy number one and I need to catch up. Let's take a smoke break."

I lit my second cigarette and handed him the lighter. For a bit of context, at that time I was trying to avoid all forms of complex thinking. It turns out there's no sustainable method for maintaining such a promise with yourself. While my brother smoked I looked down on the street bathed in amber light, thinking the way people do the night before they move across the country.

"She was a good example of that thing you always say," said my brother. "About how most of the shit in our heads gets put there on purpose by forces that want to ruin us. Or however you phrase it."

"I know what you're talking about," I said.

"For this December chick, the programming was all leaking out of her to the point where she started doing voices."

"That or she just liked talking to herself."

"But you haven't even asked what she was talking about," said my brother.

"I feel like I have a pretty good guess."

He shook his head.

"When I said she was saying some pretty reprehensible shit, I don't want you to think she was in there talking dirty," he said. "She was cursing the entire human race. I distinctly remember hearing her say 'they shouldn't be allowed to die until they've served as slaves to slaves. Slaves to lower slaves.'"

"Edgy."

He punched my knee.

"I get how it sounds, but try to actually hear it. They shouldn't be allowed to die until they've served as slaves to lower slaves? And it didn't sound like a girl doing a man's voice either. It was a man's voice coming out of her."

"I'm really hoping there's more to this story," I said.

"I can move on if you don't want to have a discussion," he said.

"I didn't ask for a discussion."

"True," he said, expelling cigarette smoke from his mouth while inhaling into his nose. "So I was standing there with her standing half naked on the bed, and I had just realized about how much of a freak she was. I was looking at her, and I remember this feeling of total disgust welling up inside me. My ears felt hot for some reason. She was yelling at me but I couldn't tell what she was saying. My eyes were locked on her lower body, I mean her crotch basically. To be fair, it was right at my eye level. She had an enormous amount of pubic hair for how small her body was, and I just couldn't bring myself to look away from it. I started to feel super embarrassed that I'd even gone in there."

"Why didn't you just walk away?" I asked.

"Listen. Before I get into this next bit, I need to make something clear," he said. "If I had told you about this when you were moving out of Mom's house, it would have made things needlessly complicated. I'm not sure you would have taken the room. You probably would have thought I was going insane. Now that you're leaving I think it's fine to tell you."

I gave him a deliberately blank look.

"I was disgusted by her for maybe ten seconds, but then I wasn't moving. I became totally fascinated by her weird looking bush. I couldn't leave the room. Something was keeping me there and I, and it felt like it was hiding in her pubes. Like a magnet or something. I didn't even think about it I just pointed between her legs and said to her, I think there's someone hiding in there. She stopped yelling and I got onto the bed. She told me there was people in there, but that didn't make it any of my business. She covered herself with her shirt. It wasn't like… it wasn't a sexual moment at that point. I wasn't even aroused necessarily, but I begged her to let me see the people. I felt drunk. She laid down and I kept begging. This is where my memory gets really foggy. At some point she had started running her fingers through my hair. After this weird back and forth she finally agreed to show me. She pulled up the edge of her shirt. Immediately, it sucked me in. The individual hairs were moving around and… vibrating, and emitting this soft almost metallic sounding melody. I put my face right in there so her crotch filled up my whole vision. She reached down, and with two fingers spread open her labia. On her inner labia I saw something that looked like a tattoo, but then I realized it was moving. It was the silhouette of a man driving a motorcycle. It kind of looked like a cartoon, or an overexposed black and white movie on her skin. And there were other figures too. Little people on her skin moving around like real people. She said they *are* real people, and when she touches herself they show up."

My expression had changed from blank to annoyed skepticism. Nonetheless, I'd just about finished my second cigarette. I'm not someone who needs to smoke everything down to the filter, so I fished out my third and held it up.

"I'm going to smoke this cig," I said. "And by the time I finish, you better tie this whole thing together."

"She started rubbing herself," he continued. "And while she was doing it her hairs started going crazy. The sound they were making was almost like music but not quite. She told me not to look away from the people. The metallic sound got louder and louder, and the little silhouettes started to move deeper inside of her vagina. Then someone came into the room. I heard footsteps behind me, and a figure knelt down on the bed beside her. In my peripheral vision it looked like a man in a brown suit."

He suddenly became serious, and he was silent for a moment, lost in thought. He continued:

"The man was talking. He said what she was doing was never going to work. I heard him say that, and I saw him there. I smelled his cologne. A man I've never seen before or since, and I swear to you he was real. She stopped rubbing herself, and she pulled my head down into her. The man was giving us instructions. I felt his hand on my back. We think we started having sex, but I don't remember the rest of it. I woke up the next morning in my car, in a parking garage down by the waterfront. I had a condom on in my pants."

"What?"

"Next thing I knew I was in the backseat of my own car. In an otherwise empty parking garage. By the waterfront. With a condom on. Under my pants."

"I'm having trouble following," I said.

"So was I," he said. "I was freaking out. You know I haven't done drugs since high school, and for the most part I'm not mentally ill. I couldn't explain it. I still can't. Have you ever woken up somewhere other than where you fell asleep?"

I set my cigarette down in the ash tray and thought about his question.

"Probably not," I said.

"That's right. It doesn't happen. I don't know how it happened," he said.

"Did she drive you there or something?"

"I don't know how it happened," he said again. "But I had to pay to get out of the garage. It was 9 a.m., and the ticket said I'd been parked there since midnight, which doesn't make sense because I know I knocked on the door a little after 3. So I drove back to the apartment. When I got home she was sitting at the table by the kitchen window eating cereal. I couldn't say anything to her. I locked my door and took a shower. Through the wall, I thought I could hear voices, like she was talking to someone, but I'd hold my breath to try to listen and the voices would stop. At that point I decided I was just going to kick her out. I didn't care if she was pissed at her roommates. I tried calling Doug so I could tell him what I was doing, but he still didn't have service, which I figured was for the best because… I mean how could I explain it? It would have sounded like I was making the worst excuse of all time for why I slept with his girlfriend."

"Anyway, before I could do anything, she knocked on my door. I rushed to put some clothes on and asked her what she wanted. She said she wanted to talk about what happened last night. I'm like *alright*, and we sat down in the living room. I remember her outfit was particularly bundled up, layers and layers of clothing. She said she wanted me to know she thought what happened last night was wrong because it wasn't fair to Doug. She wasn't going to go so far as to say I forced myself on her, but it wasn't an enjoyable experience for her. I shouldn't have invaded her privacy, and I shouldn't have taken advantage of her condition. I was like, what condition? She said she was a sub and that I knew that. That I told her what to do because I knew she couldn't say no. I told her I was pretty sure that's not what happened but she brushed me off. She said she wanted a ride back to her place. She wasn't going to tell Doug what happened if I wasn't."

"I'll bet she told him," I said.

"I wish," said my brother. "Our friendship might have been salvaged if he found out right then. But December got my phone number. She hit me up for a while after. We hooked up a few times, but it was always vanilla, and what's even weirder is that she was totally shaved. I never mentioned anything about that first night. I never asked her who the man was. She never made me do any fetish stuff. She never had me choke her. After a few weeks she sat me down again and told me we weren't sexually compatible. Then I finally told Doug what was happening. He was pissed. They broke up, and he moved out like a week later."

"How do you explain that night?" I asked. "If that actually happened…"

"I don't know how to explain it," he said. "The closest thing I have to an explanation is that this apartment must be haunted. That room is the only place in my life where I've seen something I can't explain," he said, pointing to the bedroom where I'd slept the last three years.

For a minute I continued to smoke, trying to let the story work on me. I asked myself if I'd ever seen anything out of the ordinary while I was in there. Nothing came to mind.

"I'm never going to have sex again," said my brother.

"Why's that?" I asked.

"Every time I do I'm worried someone's going to walk up behind me. It's not worth the anxiety."

We finished smoking in silence aside from the quiet motion of late-night traffic. I felt bad for my brother. Whatever had happened to him, whatever this encounter had been, it wasn't something he could tell other people. He'd have to go the rest of his life carrying this one memory. A memory almost real enough to have actually happened, but not strange enough to make him insane, and not traumatic enough to get buried beneath the reach of his thoughts.

I slept fine and moved out as planned.

He never mentioned it again.

I Waterboard Clowns
for a Living

By Flower Shop

I T has to be a scientific law, peer reviewed, shined, and waxed, that nobody likes their job. Me, personally, I'm pretty sure I hate my job more than anyone on this planet. Dead or alive throughout history. Round it up to anyone in the whole solar system. Molemen underground, colonists on the moon, Martians at home and vacationing on Pluto, whatever the hell is on Planet X, and Filipinos if they actually worked. God damn do I hate my job. You're thinking it can't be worse than the bullshit you put up with. Look, I'm sure it's rough. But I waterboard clowns for a living.

Every morning I am livid to awaken alive. Somehow my body stirs one minute before the alarm clock and every morning I check it to see there's only one minute to show time. I awake with dread and verify it is 3:00 A.M. I can always hear FX still on in the living room when I roll out of bed. I don't really shower and I don't really eat. I sleep in my sweater and I trade my pajama pants for my work jeans. After sort of splashing my face and sort of eating whatever bacon was left on the week plate I make my way to the piece of shit. The piece of shit is my car. I think the check engine light itself is broken but you don't care about any of this. In fact, I don't either.

When my car doesn't do the service of killing me on my commute I end up at work. First I would like to say I live in the city. I fucking hate the city. Humanity used to live in the forest foraging for dirt and roots to eat. We must have been desperate to get out of that life and so we built cities. Now I'm desperate to get out of the city. But I need money to pay rent and buy bacon so that I might live. That means there are clowns in need of waterboarding.

My job is on Lodi Street. Right before the bridge under perpetual construction and down the alley guarded by the Filipino kids hanging out and playing on their phones. My passenger side window can't roll all the way up so I hear them heckling me as I grind my car down the alley. What are kids doing at quarter to four in the morning in the city? Why are they up at this hour? Where are the parents? Is this the only time and place they can be on their fucking phones? These were the questions I used to ask before I accepted them like a smoker accepts the cancer in their lungs. They're just there. Deal with it.

It's 3:50 A.M. when I exit the piece of shit. Traffic is always light in the morning. The parking lot is enclosed by buildings. Most of it is wrapped by the bricks of a lab. I don't know what they do there. The east wall of this imprisoning manmade horror cocooning a pot-holed riddled parking space is my job. There are no windows. I wonder if the guys at the lab know what I do for a living.

I scan my badge at the entrance of the building. The black door to the side where I scan doesn't open. After about ten seconds of waiting I hear a buzzer. The red garage door beside the black door unlocks. It's pretty easy to lift despite the size. I enter and the nightmare begins. Inside is a miserable concrete room with pallets and wrappings containing God only knows what. Sitting on the bench at the end is my co-worker Greg.

Greg wears a bush of thick black hair on his head. He needs to shave but so do I so I never say anything. On that note, I've never heard Greg say anything once. Actually, I feel like when we started doing this I heard him speak once or twice but he must have stopped shortly after. I always get this funny feeling that if I ever met Greg outside of work he would kill me. So I guess I never heard him speak after all. But there is that dark glint in his eyes. I must have it too if I'm working here. I don't look at mirrors.

I've seen Greg's last name spelled out but I don't know how it's pronounced. I can't even remember the spelling. It's like "Bereno" or something. That isn't it but it strikes me as Italian. Make no mistake though, Greg might be a bit dark in skin but he's a full bred Slav. I just know. Below the no smoking sign I always find Greg smoking a cigarette. Smokes like a Slav. Anyways, if he can get away with having a smoke I can get away with a little time theft. At 3:51 or 3:52 A.M. I take in a deep breath of the tobacco stenched air and punch it. It's almost time to begin.

4:00 A.M. sharp and the grave shift exits from the back door. As they silently punch out, Greg and I cross into the next room. There's a restroom directly ahead. I try not to need it. On the left is the stairs heading down to our workstation. It's funny. Well, there's nothing funny about what I do but I suppose this corridor is. It's got the best lighting at work and the stairs have this thick, fuzzy carpet. It reminds me of something you would see in an 80's movie or I should just say an 80's house. Old and out of place. I call it the 80's chamber. Nobody else knows I call it that.

It's a horror show down here. I think that's the point, admittedly. A cellar a serial killer would be proud of. A boiler machine a plumber would be disgusted by. We've got plastic hanging on the walls and I've no idea what fucking for. We're not a butcher shop. The equipment might be old but I do like to imagine we're professionals at what we do by this point.

There's a couple desks at the center of the room. Filing cabinets built into them. Paperwork on top. The water hose. First thing I'll do is test that while Greg locks the door. It takes a minute to boot up the terminal. Thing must have been from the 80's like the stairs. It's really chunky and the keyboard is built into it. It hums and I sign in and enter the date. You would think it could know the date itself but no. I tap the desk indicating yeah the fucker is on and Greg goes to get the clown.

Just like the garage door I enter through there's another one down here. Greg unlocks and retrieves the clown waiting in the mantrap. Or I guess it's a clowntrap. The clown is always bound to a wheeled table. Something you would find in a hospital though we're pretty fucking far from a hospital with what we do. The clown is always awake and gagged. Always trying to break free. Always in a cold sweat wondering what the hell is going on. Well, too bad for them, Greg and I aren't very big talkers. Actually, now that I write this out, I kind of realize I don't talk too much either. At least I don't ever talk on the job. I just want to get it over with.

There's these locks between our desks on the floor. You have to wheel the table over the locks so it's over the drain. Then you attach the locks to these little mechanisms above the wheels. It's a safety precaution and amazingly one of the only things you can get written up over on the job. Always lock the wheels to the floor. I'm not exactly sure why but that's what they tell us to do. Also to double check the straps holding down the clown but Greg and I have never had a runner.

I breathe a sigh of relief when I see today's clown. The mystery behind the curtain is revealed when Greg wheels them out and locks them into place. Today's clown is a lanky one. Must be a six footer. Long arms too with skinny legs. Skinnier than Greg and I even. Let's see. He's wearing stupid fucking baggy green overalls, stupid fucking blue afro, stupid fucking purple necktie, and of course the stupid fucking red clown shoes. Those I have to measure. His shoes are eleven inches. Small for a clown.

I enter into the terminal the clown's description and the size of his shoes. Next he's ready for his shower.

First, Greg will unhinge a lock at the end of the table where the clown's head is. This will lower that end of the table alone. Once we create a sort of slope, with those stupid fucking clown shoes higher in the air, gravity is against the clown. I get the hose ready and Greg holds out the towel. I like to get the towel just a little wet. Damp but not soaked. They have to be able to breathe but that's going to change real fucking fast.

Next we ungag the clown. We've got it down to where I remove the gag right as Greg applies the towel over eyes. At this point the clown will start shouting shit like, "Please, don't do this," and, "Please let me go," and, "Please, I'll do whatever you want." Please, please, please. Please shut up, I always want to say. Today the clown's voice cracks and he cries out, "This has to be a mistake!" But there is no mistake. He was the clown left in the mantrap and I waterboard clowns for a living.

The clown raves about his family. I don't care about his stupid fucking clown family. Greg folds the towel over his mouth. The towel sort of pitches a tent because of the stupid fucking clown nose. Well, that's sort of going to make breathing harder. I shut him up and get to work. I spray the hose and suddenly, as water pours over and drenches the towel wrapped to the clown's face, he isn't as inclined to tell me about his family.

It doesn't take too long for the water to bleed through the towel. But believe me, it's going to get through and by then God will have all but abandoned the clown. The sensation of drowning is going to rip through the clown's throat like a motherfucker. That's the whole point of waterboarding. We're putting a whole fucking ocean of water between the towel and the clown's lungs. Creating a violent inability to gasp for air. It's kind of messed up, really. I'm watering him like a plant but watering plants isn't this boring.

Only a few seconds in and his chest is pounding up and down. Up and down, up and down. Like his heart must be his own graph on one of those fancy heart rate screens. I don't know what they're called, you see them at hospitals but we don't got them here. Fat chance we'd have anything that high-tech down here. The equipment I have to work with can give the piece of shit a run for its pennies.

Half a minute crawls by. I'm already ready to yawn and I know from experience the clown is ready to breathe. I'll let it rain for a few more seconds. The clown's hands are spasming like a fish out of water though I know his issue is the reverse. So I let up and up goes the towel. The clown gags, puking up water that isn't even really in him. You know, it blows my fucking mind. You would think hearing them gag like idiots would never get old but it gets old fast. In water torture it takes half a minute to break a man. Half a minute. You stand in the line at McDonald's longer than that. Half a minute and this guy is done. But me? I got eight more hours of this shit. And the kids at McDonald's think they got it bad.

Three breaths. Three rapid inhales. That's all I give them. The towel returns and the rain resumes. That's the whole trick of the gig. Figuring out when to let them breathe. When to stop the simulated drowning from genuine suffocating. It's not too hard to get it down. Half a minute, three breaths. A whole minute here and there for five breaths. It's the easiest job in the world, really. The easiest job there is and I fucking hate it. Eight hours of this! It's fucking torture. I let the clown have his three breaths and the waterboarding resumes.

Been doing this for about four years now. No idea how I lasted this long without blowing my brains out. Before that I was out of the workforce for a year. A year in customer service before that. Swear to God I thought it couldn't get worse than that but here I am. Why am I still here? I suppose the money. I mean, the pay is alright. Better than retail. Barely. It's enough so I can save up a little but the hell if I know what I'm saving up for. To escape the city and eat roots in the woods I guess. At the very least I get paid for the lunch break. I always figured that made this a government job but I never cared to look into it.

On and on the water drains. It goes through the towel but it does not come up from it until I say. It's been a minute so the clown gets his precious air for a moment. You never think how simple an affair breathing is until you've been deprived of it. You never realize the terror water can wreck until it's filled your lungs. I buy a lot of deodorant because I'm no longer comfortable showering. The sound of the water from the faucet reminds me too much of my job and I spend enough time here as it is.

Eventually the clown begins to choke on the water. They're not spitting it out. Finally, I can let my arm rest and sit for a minute while Greg performs the Heimlich. Or beat down on the clown's chest rather. That's his department. I'm sure he's broken plenty of ribs doing it but this is my chance to check my phone. Feels like my own wrist is broken having to hold that damn hose for so long.

This can interrupt the process for about fifteen minutes. Whenever the clown blacks out you have to resuscitate them. I'm proud to say in my four years I've never had a clown die on me. Maybe I'd get out of this hellhole if I hold the hose for too long. But that sounds like more trouble than it's worth. I've no idea where we get our clowns. I don't make much conversation with them if that wasn't clear enough.

My job must be a lot cooler in the movies. I'm not exactly interrogating but I'm sure on the big screen, whenever the government agent is waterboarding his clown, there's probably a lot more tension. You have to escape into your own mind to stay sane on this job. Sometimes I fantasize about getting to actually interrogate the clowns. I'll imagine myself as a movie star, asking serious questions like, "Who do you work for? How many others are crammed into the clown car? What's with the rubber chicken?" But sadly I don't ever talk to clowns.

If I'm not thinking about that I'm usually just thinking of whatever stupid shit I saw on the internet last night. Half-baked reruns in my mind's eye of boomers yelling at computers and cats leaping from horns. I wonder if the clown noses actually honk. I've never tried. Right now our current guy is bleeding from the nose. Makes it look like his clown nose popped. His eyes are pretty bloodshot too. That's another thing. A clown, or anyone I guess, can look like a corpse but still have a long way to go.

Another part of my job is recording the process of waterboarding and how it affects the clown. Whoever is getting my reports really wants to know how the makeup holds up throughout. You would be surprised by some of these fellas. Clowns can really come in all shapes and sizes and even colors. Once in a while you get a clown whose paint is effectively bleached onto their skin. Hours of waterboarding and it doesn't come off. That's some dedication. Got the paint off this guy though. Now he's just pale because of all the vomiting.

We're giving him a few minutes as he stirs. His brain must be fried. It'll be like dumping water on exposed circuits in a minute though. For now, it's deep breaths and unsynchronized blinking. Looks like he pissed himself too. I'd feel bad for him but look at 'em. He gets to lay down and my feet are already killing me. Seven more hours to go.

The next three hours will be just like the first. Just as the last day was like the last four years of this shit. At 8:00 A.M. I'm saved by the bell. Toss the towel over the clown's watery eyes and hang up the hose for half an hour. The break room is just a room over. My kitchen is nicer and I've got ants crawling up the walls. TV isn't even right either. It's got this blue fucking hue to it that drives me nuts. Four departments at work. Recovery, Waterboarding, Audit, and Maintenance. Maintenance never does its damn job.

Greg packs a lunch and has a smoke. I just need a coffee and a chance to unwind. Always French vanilla. Love the French. I only really eat lunch though so that'll be after work. I'll check my phone and scroll through the news. A big shooting in Philadelphia today. I was there once. City was fucking filthy. Must have been a homeless person on every corner. Made me wonder where they all came from. Just like the clowns work wrangles up. I'm sure I'll never know. Oh look, my own city is trending with its own shooting. Not as big it seems but at a school. I actually went to community college myself. I've got a business degree though you would never guess it looking at me. What the hell do I even need it for with drowning clowns? And just like that I blinked and the break is over.

There's always a bit of suspense coming back from break. Did the clown get out? Maybe it sounds silly but I do worry a little about it. Like maybe the clown escaped and it'll be like the movies again. The clown will be waiting at the side of the door and bash Greg's head in with that fire extinguisher we need to replace. Then he takes me by surprise and drowns me with my own hose. But alas. There he is still on the table. Fucking useless. I should know better. Four hours under the hose and you're not up for a fight.

I grab the hose and hear a mutter. A very sad and broken mutter. "P-please… you don't have to do this." The clown is all but whispering. Greg's not even looking as he returns the towel. "I… I'll do anything. Just make it stop. Make it stop and I'll… I'll… whatever… stop…"

He'll do anything? "Anything you want," he mutters again as if he read my mind. Anything at all? Can he make the hands on the clock say 12:00 P.M. and free me from this place? No. He can't. So he gets the water.

At least three more hours to go. Would I stop if the clown could pull a million dollars out of his polka-dot top hat or suitcase of props? Fuck me. What would I even do with that much money? Buy the joke shop? Doesn't matter. He can't do shit. He can't even breathe.

This one is about done talking. A lot of times you'll get clowns rambling, trying to say anything to get you to stop. They'll even tell you their names in some sort of attempt to appeal to your sense of mercy. How the hell can I take them seriously? Your name was Bubbles. Do you want me to laugh or feel sorry? My landlord doesn't have mercy for me so I have none for them.

Don't think I'm cruel or anything. It's just a job. I'm anything but cruel. I don't walk out here and say things like, "Hey! You feeling thirsty, buddy? Well drink up!" No way I'm like that. I'm very professional about all this. I don't make small talk. I'm just here to do my job.

The job's almost over too. At least for the day. Usually around 11:30 A.M. Greg and I will start to clean up our mess. Another day of not hanging myself with my own fucking hose. The waterboarding is over and thank God. I can go home.

I submit my report as Greg mops up the blood. You don't leave scars on the clowns with this job. Not physically. I can't imagine what's happened to their minds, how they've changed from the clown they were when we wheeled them out here. So typically I don't think about it. But today I do Greg the favor and wheel our clown back to the mantrap. I take one last at him. He looks like a vegetable. With a chill I'm reminded it is time for lunch.

No idea what happens next for the clown when we lock 'em back up. Maybe day shift has their go at him next. Or maybe they have their own clown ready to go. I never asked and frankly I don't care to. That's another thing too. We never work the same clown twice. What happens to them when the shift is over I don't know. What I do know is I'm always excited to get out of here and that's where my mind is today.

I say goodbye to Greg with the sound of me punching out. No words exchanged. Perhaps never will there be. We don't make eye contact as we exit the building. I return to the piece of shit and discover the Filipinos are gone. Unfortunately, they've been replaced with traffic. It's noon now and everyone is on their break when I'm just getting out.

Before I head home there is one last item I should describe in my routine. For this is the item plunged deep into my chest, bleeding my heart, drowning me in misery. Of course you already know it's a girl. I don't see her every day and I'm sure it's not fair to call it love. But I like this girl. I like to look at her and watch her work if only for a little while.

I can only catch this girl in the wild but I know at least one of her habitats and that's where I go for lunch. Or rather the shitty sub shop next to where she performs. Every day I work I stop by this place called "The Sub Hub." A subway knockoff but it is right beside the actual subway station entrance and I was always amused by that stupid detail. I order the foot long with turkey, lettuce, and American cheese. I tell the lady to, "Drown it in vinegar." I get a look for that. She might hate her job but she doesn't have a clue what I do for a living.

I'm in luck today. I'm in wonderful luck. The girl I like is next door. I was worried the incident across town might have prevented her from being here but I guess things are quiet on this side of the city. I sit down with my sub and cola, pretending not to be watching her but I am. She's performing as she occasionally does in front of the joke shop. Now we've reached the point as to why I actually decided to write all this. You see, the girl is a performer. A clown. A jester, technically. I don't know the finer details or any of that stuff. But she's dressed in a full piece suit and the best I can describe it is as a juggler you would expect to see in a Medieval court. Not a clown. Different. She's different from a clown.

I just think she's cute. Is that so fucking wrong? Am I not allowed to think that? My job doesn't define me. It's not my whole life. It's already too much of my life. I can like who I want and she's not even a clown. She's a jester. A street performer. She waves a sign around saying come check the shop out for God's sake. She's not going to children's birthday parties, touching or killing kids or whatever the hell the real clowns do.

She's cute, I would guess she's of French stock, and nothing comes closer in this world to making me smile than her. I can't actually smile, mind you. I can't even stomach the hope of having a relationship with this creature but damn it I paid for my sub and she dances over there with the intention of having an audience. You know what really makes her special? What truly makes me admire her? She breaks all the rules of scientific law. She dresses up like a fucking idiot and you know what? She looks like she loves her job. What a specimen.

Yes, we have never interacted. I've never been caught staring by her. It's fun to think she would notice me one day and we hit it off but this isn't a movie. It never works like the movies. No, I just stare and watch her work a little while. I'm harmless. I'll finish my meal and hope she's back again tomorrow. But when I go home, when I watch a movie where the unreal is real, when I go to bed she will be there. She will be there with my closing thoughts, filling me with dread. Begging the question again, will I find her at the table at work tomorrow?

I awake by the dread of the alarm clock. I fall asleep to the dread of wonder. I wonder much in my life. Like if I were to bump into her outside could she break the spell of my life and free me from my torment? But this is nothing like the movies. This is real life and in real life I waterboard clowns.

The Marlinspike

By Miles MacNaughton

I.

MIKE Hanson watched his son splash in the lake. His wife lounged on a towel next to him, sunglasses on, tanning in the warm sunlight. A tame wind shuffled through the trees. Hanson sipped from a small glass of rum, read a line in his book, then looked at the lake. Another line, another look.

"You should rest," Maggie said. "You were up all night."

"Once he comes in for lunch."

"He'll be out there for at least another hour. Take a rest."

"No," Hanson said. "I better keep an eye on him."

"I'm watching him."

Hanson glanced at his wife who was watching the inside of her eyelids. He didn't say anything and when he glanced back at the lake, his son was missing. The water was eerily still. Hanson snapped his book closed and started to rise but a second later his son breached and whipped his hair around and wiped his face. He was grinning at a little object in his hand—a treasure fished from the bottom of the lake. Hanson let out a ragged sigh.

"You weren't watching him," he said.

"Mmm," said Maggie, turning on her stomach. "I'm sure he's fine."

Hanson carefully opened his book but couldn't read a line. Every splash yanked him into the lake. Every dive stole his breath until Bobby returned. The water lapped agonizingly at the shore, thin and foamless and colored like lapis lazuli. Hanson closed his book again. "After lunch he's putting on his floaties."

"Honey."

"Well, you know what"—Hanson tossed his hands at the lake—"if he goes down and I can't see him, what am I supposed to do?"

Maggie was sitting up now. "You've got to trust him a little more."

"I trust him just fine."

"You taught him to swim yourself, and we're right here if he needs us. Besides"—Maggie pushed her sunglasses down her nose—"who's idea was this?"

"Mine," Hanson muttered.

Maggie's face softened and she laid a hand on her husband. "I know it's hard. Reggie was a long time ago, on an ocean a thousand miles away. Bobby loves swimming. He loves the water! You can't hold him back from the things he loves."

"I know," Hanson said guiltily.

They shared a smile and then a kiss, and Maggie started to lay back down and Hanson started to reach for his book, and as they did, they both looked at the lake. It was completely still. Bobby was gone. Maggie only half-paused, but Hanson froze completely. They waited.

"Bobby?" Maggie called.

Bobby emerged slowly from the water as if he'd been listening, his eyes glossy and mouth slightly open. Hanson knew that look. He was drowning. Hanson leapt to his feet and dove into the lake. He reached Bobby in a moment and the boy fell feebly into his arms. By the time they reached land, Bobby was coughing up the water in his lungs and looking around in confusion. Maggie hurriedly wrapped him in a towel and dried him off.

"I'm okay," Bobby said when the excitement died down. "My foot just got caught."

"Oh, look at that rash," Maggie cooed, holding Bobby's leg in her hands. "Wait here and I'll get the med kit from the car."

"I'll watch him," Hanson said. Maggie gave him an odd look before she left, as if what he said was nonsense. Hanson rubbed his son's shoulders. "You alright?"

The boy shrugged. He looked shaken. He probably wouldn't swim for the rest of the day. Bobby fidgeted with something in his hands, catching Hanson's attention. He nodded to it, hoping to put Bobby's mind off the event. "What did you find?"

"A stick," Bobby said. He showed him what he'd fished from the lake: a thin metal rod with a thick knob on one end.

"Well, well," Hanson said, gently taking the tool. "This is a marlinspike. I used to use these to splice rope. See that flat tip? You drive it into rope to split the threads. Then you can tie two ropes together."

"Why can't you just tie the ropes together?"

"If you break the bonds of each rope first, they hold together better. It makes the whole rope stronger." Hanson inspected the tool for a moment. "We better not keep this. It's pretty rusty."

"But I found it."

"I'll get you a new one from the tackle shop."

Before Bobby could complain, Maggie returned with the med kit and set about fussing with the rash on her son's leg. Hanson stood and walked to the edge of the lake with the marlinspike in his fist. He thoughtlessly thumped it in his palm, and eventually he could no longer keep his gaze away, and his eyes turned to the three initials etched on the cone: MJH, Michael James Hanson. In the back of his mind, he saw the rash on Bobby's leg: four long red lines and a stumpy fifth, as if he'd been grabbed by a hand. On the top of his son's foot had been a very dark bruise, the thought of which made Hanson queasy.

Hanson threw the marlinspike far into the lake and watched as it splashed and sank into the deep.

That night, Hanson went to his usual bar and took rum with the other usuals. He bought drinks and talked to whoever would listen. The night waxed on and Hanson filled up, never delirious, incessantly and unusually chatty. A close eye would have spotted the extra tightness in his lips, the strangely loud voice, the searching flurry of his eyes. Something was eating at him, corroding his nerves. Eventually he was the only one in the bar and the hour had turned to the single digits. Without company his good mood left him, and he quietly sipped at his nearly empty glass of rum. The bartender patiently polished a glass with a clean rag. "Getting pretty late," he said. "Want anything for the road, Mike?"

"I probably shouldn't." Hanson pressed the glass to his forehead. "You think I'm good?"

The bartender shrugged.

Hanson glared, annoyed at the indifference, and even more annoyed at his own disheveled reflection in the mirror behind the bar. His wife was going to give him an earful when he got home. Bobby woke up on the car ride home, complaining about his bruise and his rash, and about a dream where someone drowned him in a lake. Hanson suspected it was the first of many future nightmares—something he was now responsible for. That damn lake and its cold, blue water. Hanson remembered the last time he'd been on the ocean, the last time he'd been in anything deeper than a bathtub. And that old marlinspike with his initials, as if he'd seen it yesterday, not ten years ago. The rum and regret hit him from belly to brain.

"I shouldn't have taken him out there," Hanson groaned.

The bartender nodded; he'd already heard the story. "Last call."

Hanson nodded too, but his mind was far from Bobby. Those initials, MJH, etched in his own hand. Last time he saw that thing, it was sinking into the Pacific. Hanson set his glass down. "It's just the strangest thing," he said to no one in particular. The alcohol was fogging his brain, but it couldn't fully flush the unwanted memories. He needed more. "I'll take that last round, I think."

The bartender poured out the rum and stoppered the bottle. "You finish that, and I'll close up the back."

Hanson sipped at his rum and the bartender tossed his towel over his shoulder and stepped through the kitchen doors. Hanson swirled the rum in his glass and watched the alcohol stick to the sides and crawl back down. Swirl, stick, crawl, drink. On the side of the glass was a little pirate's skull with two swords crossed under the stiffly grinning jaw. The old shanty earwormed into his mind.

"Fifteen men on a dead man's chest," he crooned, transfixed by the glittering rum. "Yo ho ho and a bottle of rum." He sipped. "Drink and the devil had done for the rest…"

His eyes fell on the mirror, and with dim surprise he saw that he was no longer alone in the bar. A man in a dark coat was hunched over the table behind him, his back to the mirror, one arm tucked under his face, the other extended with an empty glass in his hand. A nameless feeling crept up Hanson's spine. A presence lingered, as if someone hovered over his shoulder. It was utterly silent in the room, and Hanson was unwilling to turn his eyes from the body that had appeared behind him. The more he stared, the more his anxiety grew. The shape was too familiar.

Hanson hoped for the bartender to come through any moment and save him the trouble of rousing his immobile companion, but as soon as his eyes drifted to the kitchen double-doors, the light inside went out with a click, and the only other light came from the small bulbs under the bar mirror. He glanced in the mirror, hoping that he was simply drunk and alone, and yet the unmoving man remained as he was, perceivable even in the grim dark. Hanson drew a slow sip from his glass to calm his nerves. He suddenly coughed and spit it out on the bar. The rum had turned to brine. He looked at the glass in his hand, then dropped it with a cry. The inside bloomed with algae.

The glass rolled on the bar and stopped against a limp arm.

A man sat next to Hanson, his face pressed into the bar, his jaw agape, his skull caved in above the left eye. Sitting in a pool of blood on the table was the eye itself, white and gleaming and staring into space. Hanson was back on his ship in the Pacific, the rain rattling against the thin windows, salt and copper scenting the cabin air, Reggie dead at the table, a half-finished glass of rum filling his fingers, a surprised stare leveled at the wall, and a bloodied marlinspike in Hanson's hand.

Hanson launched himself away, and as his vision steadied he saw that the bar seat was empty and the bartender had returned from the kitchen. Hanson's ship was gone, sold long ago, and the Pacific Ocean blissfully far away. Together they retreated to the parking lot, Hanson lingering in the yellow pools cast by the overhead lights, speaking senselessly and trying to revive earlier conversations. The bartender left him in the dark. Hanson drove home with the lights on in his car, and he thought of his ship, of the Pacific, of a night swallowed by a storm.

II.

IT was ten years ago that Reggie and Hanson planned for a three-day fishing trip over a long weekend. There was a chance of storms on the second night; it was otherwise clear weather. In the morning of their departure the seagulls cawed in answer to the dull honk of the albatross. The glassy surface of the Pacific parted easily for Hanson's ship. The northwest sea was black as night and thick like syrup. Hanson's boat cast a cold shadow from the icy pinprick of sunlight rising in the east.

Hanson kept the helm in his grasp and Reggie in his sights. The man had been flaunting his happiness ever since he started dating their mutual friend, Maggie—a woman Hanson had been dating until recently. In truth, Hanson held no ill will toward the man. Reggie and Maggie had grown up together. Their dates were cute, but in time, Maggie would leave him for another man. She might even go back to Hanson. That was just her nature. She was loose, but he loved her.

Hanson shook himself out of his thoughts as Reggie mounted

the stairs. "How's she driving?" Reggie asked.

"Smooth," Hanson said. "It's going to be a perfect weekend for fishing."

Reggie sighed and leaned on the gunwale railing. "Maggie would love this view."

Hanson grunted, unwilling to broach the obvious topic. Reggie cleared his throat and tried again. "She keeps asking when you're going to take her deep-sea fishing, you know. I think she'd love it."

Hanson nodded and kept his eyes on the sea.

"You should see her fish on the lake," he continued. "She really is a natural."

"Come on," Hanson said. "This is a guy's weekend. I don't want to talk about women."

"Buddy, it's all we ever talk about on guy weekends." Reggie laughed and looked out at the onyx sea and slowly let his smile fall away. He took a breath to gather his courage. "I want you to know that I'm going to propose to her," he said.

Hanson stared at Reggie as if he'd been shot. "What? When?"

"Next week. You know how next week we're going down to San Francisco? I'm going to do it at the Golden Gate, where you used to take her. It's her favorite spot."

"I know it is," Hanson said. "I dated her too."

"And I'm marrying her," Reggie said. He was smiling. A hot flash went through Hanson's chest, but he tried to roll with the banter.

"Is this why you wanted to go fishing? Just to make fun of me?"

"No, no. You embarrassed yourself enough with Maggie. I really just wanted to fish with you. We may not see each other much when I'm married. I want to have a good time before then."

"You really think she's going to say yes?" Hanson said, still trying to get one over.

"Absolutely," Reggie said, "given all the other things I've gotten her to say yes to."

The jab stuck in Hanson's throat, and despite waiting for him to continue, Reggie did not. He merely left, still grinning, and descended into the cabin. Hanson stared at the ocean. Thoughts of Maggie rattled around, memories of their former life together. He remembered the feeling of a wedding ring in his hand, and his own stupidity months later when he returned it, unused and ungiven. It hadn't been long until Reggie picked her up, and it didn't take long to realize how much happier Maggie looked with Reggie. He tried to be happy for them, but he couldn't help his resentment. The only thing Hanson feared more than Maggie saying yes to Reggie was seeing an invitation to the wedding of the girl he had loved and lost. His dissociation festered into anger, which boiled into hate. Hanson gripped the helm and set his jaw and stared at the glassy ocean in furious quiet.

That night, Hanson laid in his bunk staring at his snoozing shipmate. His thoughts darkened with the night. Maybe there was a chance to hook up with Maggie before she married. Maybe he could get her to have his child instead of Reggie's, and it would be their secret, one they'd never tell. Then he thought he could get Maggie back if he beat Reggie in a fight, but it was a pointless thought. As much as he could not fully allow himself to admit it, Reggie was the better man. Maggie had chosen the better man and Hanson knew it. He knew she would say yes when Reggie proposed. Hopeless frustration mounted in his heart and he dreamed of beating Reggie in bare-knuckle combat and taking back his woman. He'd smash that man to pieces. He'd leave him dead on the ground and let the birds pick him clean.

The longer he thought about the imagined fight, the more realistic his thoughts became. The animal rage crystalized into clinical spite, and that soon turned to thoughts of murder. It was an ugly truth, but the only thing standing between him and Maggie was a very killable man. With Reggie out of the way, Maggie would come back to him. She would have no one else to love. Then he could propose, and she'd say yes and be his forever. But how to do it? There were no guns on his ship. Smothering would be too difficult. Their filet knife came to mind, but unless he killed Reggie immediately, he'd likely be stabbed himself. Hanson's nebulous, murderous thoughts kept him up for another hour before his brain finally sent him to sleep.

In the morning he only half-remembered his intent and felt shame on the back of his ears. Reggie was a good friend and had been for many years, and Hanson was no murderer. Over breakfast, however, as Reggie once again alluded to his future with Maggie in that superior, gloating tone which set Hanson's teeth on edge, murder again filled his mind. By noon, he had convinced himself that the task was inevitable. It wasn't that he wanted Reggie to suffer. He just wanted him out of the way, and murder was the only option. There was no choice in the matter. The man had become a nuisance. His smile and laugh were intolerable, and the continuous blows to Hanson's pride over that agonizing day were too much to bear. Reggie's every action mocked him and insulted his manhood, from handing him the bait can, to offering to fill up his rum glass, to congratulating Hanson when he pulled in an eight incher while the sixteen incher Reggie caught flopped about in their livewell. Reggie doted on Hanson like an older brother begrudgingly stringing him along on a fishing trip meant for the big kids, and it made him sick with disgust.

That evening Hanson was alone on the deck, splitting rope with his marlinspike and watching the storm clouds roll in from the west in tall, thick bundles like fistfuls of cauliflower. Silent ribbons of distant lightning slashed in the purple dark, and the sporadic gusts of wind grated on his nerves. Eventually Hanson went down into the cabin in the hopes of pouring himself a drink. Reggie was already at their breakfast booth with an open bottle of rum in his fist. He grinned when he saw Hanson.

"There he is!" he shouted. "Come to drink, finally? God damn, what an absolutely beautiful storm it'll be. Cheer up, Hanson! You look terrible. You know what you need? A little rum." Reggie poured a sloshing amount into a glass, then passed it to his shipmate and took a deep gulp for himself. "And one for me. When's the game on? We getting any signal on the box?"

Reggie got up and tuned their satellite TV and thumped it a few times. Hanson's blood pressure spiked with each oafish rap. Eventually the baseball game from the coast came trickling through and Reggie collapsed onto the couch with the rum bottle in hand. For the next two hours he was belligerent and loud, shouting at the TV for no reason and throwing the couch pillows at it when a player struck out. Hanson warned him against hitting his equipment; Reggie just chuckled and drank more rum. When the game ended, Reggie opened a new bottle and sat in their little breakfast booth with what he claimed was his final glass. Hanson knew what that meant. He steeled himself for the mopey, emotional attempt at a heart-to-heart.

"I can't believe it," Reggie murmured. "Me, married. I never thought I'd ever… I mean, someday, of course. Someday it'd just happen. But with Maggie? A dream. A dream come true."

"You don't have to tell me," Hanson said venomously.

"She talks about you sometimes. She tells me all the stuff you liked to do." Reggie's eyes were soft. "She liked you, man. She really did. It's a shame you let her go."

A hot flash went through Hanson's neck; he definitely did not let Maggie go, and not two months later, she was dating Reggie. He eyed the glass in Reggie's hand and wondered if he could get the man to drink himself to death. "It is a shame!" he said as he poured his friend another glass and slid into the opposite seat of the booth. "But she's with the better man now, isn't she? Come on, have a drink with me."

"Oh, I think I've had enough." Reggie pushed his glass away, then perked up. "Better man, you said?"

"Yes, yes. The better man. Come on, you can't pretend you don't see it yourself?" Hanson's eyes burned. "You're stronger than me. Better looking. You've got the better job, the better house, a nice car—you're a god damn stud! And you've got the girl of both our dreams. How is that not a reason to celebrate? Drink up, Reg. Go on, drink it all."

"I must have had six already," he slurred.

"Then a drink to marriage!" Hanson said. "Come on, don't

tell me you're not going to celebrate that?"

Reggie came alive and seized the glass. "Yes, to marriage!" he shouted. "God damn, yes! To women and to marriage! Oh my God, Hanson. I'm going to marry Maggie. I'm going to make her my wife."

Hanson's tight smile flared. "Yes, you are. Congratulations."

"You know what I'm going to do? On our first night, right after the wedding, I'm gonna"—Reggie motioned pulling something down, then spreading something with his hands— "and I'm gonna do it all night long." He thrust his hips sloppily into the table.

"Is that so?" Hanson said brightly. He stood and moved out of the booth. "Let's have another toast."

Reggie chuckled. He was thinking of something else.

Hanson had only made it a few steps. Something in that lusty chuckle felt like a final insult. Something terrible kicked into his throat. He felt the marlinspike in his waistband. Hanson yanked it free and smashed it into the back of Reggie's head.

The man groaned, and as he slumped he tried to steady himself with his free hand. Hanson grabbed Reggie by the shoulder, raised his weapon in triumph, then brought it down and knocked Reggie's head into the table. He seized the marlinspike with both hands and slammed down again and again, increasing his speed with each blow, and with a sudden and sickening crack Reggie's face fractured and the bone splintered like shattered glass. Hanson paused, bloodlust fogging his eyes.

"All night, huh?" Hanson shouted, brandishing the weapon. "Is that right? All night?!" He grabbed the marlinspike with both hands and smashed it down, spurting blood all over his clothes, then he smashed down a second time, and then with one final blow he let out a thunderous yell.

He stumbled back, then settled onto the couch to calm his heart. Reggie's skull was completely caved in, his jaw open in a gasp, his tongue lolling out in a pool of his own blood, his left eye popped out of its socket and gazing vacantly at the open air, one arm stretched out with a glass in hand, the other loosely under his head. Hanson stared at Reggie for a few seconds and waited for him to close his eyes and groan and rub his head or turn the other way and start laughing. But nothing happened. The man's disfigured, gaping face stared at him in empty silence.

Hanson looked around the room while his brain gorged itself on endorphins. He suddenly found it hard to think about anything for more than a moment. The insistent urge to hide the body grew, but he couldn't bear to look at it. It took a concentrated effort to stand, and when he did, his legs wobbled and his stomach swelled into his larynx. Hanson paced and swore at the dead man. He mocked him, he ranted at him, he blamed him for leaving him no choice but murder. The smashed face and dead eyes received the words with deaf indifference. Outside, thunderheads swallowed the sunset.

Hanson dragged the body from the cabin, weighed it down, and pitched it into the waves. With a mighty hurl he launched the marlinspike into the ocean. He threw out the life preserver as well, then cleaned the cabin. He took a break only to drive the ship around in the early part of the storm, just in case someone investigated the black box, and then he finished cleaning, dropped anchor, and crawled into his bunk as the rain began drumming on the windowpanes.

Hanson folded his hands over his stomach and looked at the ceiling and thought lightly that he was a murderer. It hadn't fully set in, but it rounded in his mind several times that he had killed someone. He felt like a schoolboy who had done something he knew was wrong and knew exactly how he was going to be caught. He decided to keep his story simple. There was no murder. Reggie got drunk and fell off the side of the boat in the middle of the storm, and despite the life preserver being tossed overboard, plus a search of his own in the rain, no sign of Reggie could be found. The situation felt unreal. What if they scanned his boat for evidence? What if they found the blood? No—he would find a way. Jail was not an option. Maggie was waiting for him.

Eventually, Hanson turned on his side and tried to find sleep, yet for the rest of that rumbling night a clear image of Reggie's gaping jaw and wide-open eyes lingered in his mind. He tossed fitfully in the storm, dreaming of a dead man with a fractured face crawling over the gunwale with a marlinspike in hand.

III.

IT was late when Hanson made it home from the bar. Though he tried, sleep always stayed a pace away from him. Maggie murmured something over her shoulder after one too many sighs and tosses, and it drove Hanson out of his bed and down the stairs into the kitchen for an untimely nightcap. He took his drink out to the mosquito-netted patio which was adorned with deck chairs, a well-used grill, and a variety of boy-sized aquatic gear for fishing and kayaking. Just outside on a paver extension was a tidy outdoor dining set and firepit. The little burglar light came on as he settled into a deck chair and sipped. A distant wind cut through the backyard shadows, the first warning of an inbound thunderhead, and it whistled hollowly through the netting. In the absence of thunder, the eerily silent lightning set his nerves on a razor's edge.

"Storm's coming," he muttered to no one in particular, and he raised his glass to drink.

A light clink of glass answered him.

His nightcap stopped an inch from his lip. In the corner of his eye was the heaped shadow of a man slumped over at his dining set, one arm tucked underneath his head, one arm stretched out, a twinkling glass in his hand. The little pool of light shed by the patio lamp stopped just shy of the thing in the dark. A chill crawled up his spine.

Hanson cursed quietly at the thing, and then he hurled a bevy of curses, of insults. He boasted about his wife, about his son and the house they lived in, about how many times he'd pounded that girl. He relentlessly mocked the motionless figure lurking in the dark. But as he railed, his anger became a thin mask for a creeping fear. At the lake, anything was bound to the water's edge.

At the bar, whatever happened ended at his car door. There was no such guarantee in his own house, on his own property, that whatever invasive terror would stop at the kitchen door. Fear poisoned his mind. Eventually his patience wore out. Rising to his feet, Hanson shouted, "Damn it, for the love of God, say something!"

As he watched in horror, the dead man in the dark slowly sat up.

Hanson ran indoors and slammed the patio door behind him. Good God!—he must be losing his mind. He couldn't shake the urge to find a weapon. Hanson ran for the knife drawer and yanked it open. Not a knife was to be found; they were all replaced with marlinspikes, the initials MJH carved into the handle. Hanson backed away in horror, and then the patio deck creaked. The burglar light flickered listlessly and a shadow slowly pooled on the curtain over the patio door. There could be no doubt that a dead man stood inches behind that thin pane of glass, that little strip of floral curtain. The handle jiggled. Hanson pressed himself against the wall. The patio light flickered, then left the kitchen in the dark.

There was silence, and then there was the creak of something moving across his deck. The shadow crept across the kitchen window. A flash of lightning in the distance silhouetted a broken body. Not a sound came from beyond. A hand pressed into the glass. It wanted to get inside.

A presence bloomed at Hanson's right. Maggie stood in the hallway. She was nearly bare in her pastel pink bathrobe, her hair puffy and her eyes still shedding sleep. She came around the doorframe with a tentative step, wrapping her robe around her waist and leaning in as if she expected Hanson to be making breakfast. She stopped when she saw her husband pressed against the wall.

"Mike?" Maggie whispered. "What's going on?"

She followed her husband's gaze to the kitchen window and saw the thing behind the glass. Fear entered her eyes. She froze. For a brief moment Hanson met the eyes of his wife, and when they returned their gazes to the window, the figure was gone. Hanson pushed off from the wall, then boldly went to the window and looked out. His yard was empty. A bolt of thin, silent lightning streaked across the sky.

"Who was that?" she said. "Should we call the police?"

Something smashed through glass nearby, and seconds later there were chirping cries of terror from a nearby bedroom.

Another glance between them, and then Maggie went hurtling toward Bobby's room. Hanson stumbled after her as the hallways pitched around him. He was back on his boat in the Pacific in the middle of a storm, tossing about in his bed as he dreamed of undead crawling over the gunwale. Brine filled his nose. More cries, followed by Maggie's screams. He leaned himself against Bobby's doorframe: Maggie was stretched across the bed, nearly halfway out the window, with both hands wrapped around the flailing legs of their son.

Hanson shot across the room and grabbed Maggie by the waist and pulled. It was like trying to drag a freighter. His wife cried and begged incoherently. Hanson dug in his heels and took three strong steps back, and Bobby's waist moved back in. A black, slime-covered arm was wrapped firmly under the boy's arms.

Maggie cried. Bobby kept kicking and her fingers were slipping. Her son retreated slowly into the dark, and then her grip failed and he vanished through the broken window.

"No!" she cried. "Bobby, come back! Bobby!" She wrenched herself free from Hanson's grip and fell through the glass. Her shouts echoed through the back yard and into the neighbor's. Her voice went shrill, then faded as she ran into the night.

But Hanson did not follow her. He sat in Bobby's room staring at the windowsill. There, sitting in a little pool of blood, a single lonely eye stared at him in dead, indifferent silence.

Stampede of the Protestants

By Zulu Alitspa

IT was the broken drier which brought the convenience store to his attention. Greg had woken up in front of his television, and then heard the noise of his drier. It was after midnight, and he had put the clothes in right after dinner. It should have already shut off, but it was still going. And so he got up from the couch, made his way through the kitchen, and entered the laundry room. And there was the door.

A simple glass door, with a steel handle across the middle, just like you'd find at any normal convenience store. At the back of his laundry room. Glancing down, he opened the drier to trigger the automatic shut-off. He had expected the door to be gone when he looked back up, but it was still there. His first instinct was that he was in the wrong house, but then he glanced around. It was his washer, his drier, and his brand of laundry powder sitting on the one shelf. The normal sink was there, and a quick glance through the narrow window at the top of the room revealed the same view of the same parking lot, with mostly the same cars, that he'd been seeing for over two years now.

There was nothing to do but check the new door. It was seamlessly integrated into the drywall of the room, and narrower than it should have been. A bit shorter, too. Greg would have needed to crouch down and turn sideways to squeeze through. Naturally, he tried to open it. The door did not give, not even with the minor click of a deadbolt hitting its frame. He looked down to a sign posted on the inside of the glass.

CLOSED

The hours were listed. Eight in the morning until eight at night. He pressed his face to the door, using his hands to shield against a nonexistent glare. He could make out two shelves looming over a narrow walkway, but the details eluded him. He stepped back and stood up, once again examining his laundry room to ensure that he was in the right apartment.

This is normal, he thought. A trick of the light. It must be. I am mistaking normal things for strange doors.

Greg was not able to sleep, and when he got out of bed the next morning, he immediately went into the laundry room to check on the door. Still there. Still CLOSED. Except, with the daylight coming through the window, he could see inside. The two shelves were lined with merchandise: instant soups and coffee, packaged chips and candy bars. At the far end of the aisle was a checkstand. Advertisements festooned the back wall behind the register, and a dainty cigarette case was mounted to the ceiling.

He called out of work and returned to the laundry room to wait until the sign said OPEN. It was nearly eight in the morning. The employee should be here shortly to unlock the door and explain what was happening. Greg split his attention between the laundry room and the front door of his apartment, wondering if some business was actually sending its employees through his living room in order to spend twelve hours waiting for a customer to show up in his laundry room. It was possible, he decided, that someone had been working here for months. The door wasn't easy to spot in the daytime. He himself left for work at seven-thirty in the morning. But, then again, he was usually home before eight and he would have seen them leaving.

Four hours later, he decided to get lunch. As soon as he stepped outside of his front door, he remembered a critical piece of the puzzle. He lived in an apartment complex. He had a next door neighbor. Theoretically, the bulk of the convenience store was in his neighbor's laundry room. Greg did not know his neighbor, and assumed he was at work, but decided to knock anyway. After a few seconds, a suspicious voice answered through the door.

"Who is it?"

"My name is Greg. I'm your neighbor."

He listened as the locks were unfastened, and a white-haired man opened the door, wearing a pair of slacks with a polo shirt tucked neatly into the waistband. Clean cut and prim, he gave off the impatient vibe of a resentfully-retired technician.

"Nice to meet you," said the man, offering his hand for a shake. "My name is Tom."

Greg nodded as the man seized his weak grip and pumped it once.

"So, uh—"

He wasn't quite sure how to start this conversation. Tom picked up the pause.

"Have you noticed anything weird going on in your apartment?"

Greg sighed with relief.

"Yeah," he said. "That's an understatement. I came over here to ask you the same thing."

"What's happening in your apartment?"

"As near as I can tell," said Greg, "someone has opened a convenience store in my laundry room."

Tom nodded. Greg continued.

"Same thing at your place?"

"Not exactly," said Tom. "Would you like to come and look?"

Greg looked over his shoulder. Tom's apartment was a bit untidy, but otherwise it looked like the apartment of a sane and normal man. Tom led him back to the laundry room, where there was another small, glass door.

"Have you tried to open it?" asked Greg. Tom shrugged.

"Of course. Apparently it's closed."

Greg knelt down and looked through the glass, peering beyond the CLOSED sign. At the back was a counter and cash register, just like in his. Except instead of shelves of merchandise, there was a single narrow counter running alongside the wall, with three small stools. He squinted at the area behind the counter. A display tacked to the backboard showed a choice of pizzas: extra-large, large, medium, and small.

He stood back up and looked at Tom.

"It's a pizza parlor."

Tom nodded, his arms folded across his chest as he furrowed his brow and tapped his toe on the linoleum.

"I don't even eat pizza. Are we going insane?"

It suddenly occurred to Greg that he had never seen Tom before in his life. What if no one had actually answered the door at all? What if he was suffering from psychosis, and had simply imagined a neighbor in an empty, unlocked apartment? No normal person wears dress shoes inside their own house. Greg was starting to get nervous. He looked back towards the front door.

"Let's go talk to the building manager," he said.

If Tom was a hallucination, he probably would have wanted to avoid disproving himself, and so Greg was relieved when Tom immediately agreed to let a third party into the situation. They took a walk down the stairs and found a line of people waiting outside the manager's office. They joined the queue, and the last woman in line turned to them. She tugged her bathrobe tighter and smirked.

"I have a laundromat in my laundry room," she said, clearly pleased with the irony of it.

"I've got a pizza parlor," said Tom, and then he jerked his

head slightly to indicate Greg.

"And he's got a convenience store."

The woman smiled.

"Well, at least your thing is useful. Have you managed to get inside?"

"We haven't even tried," said Greg. "Or, at least I haven't. I mean, I jiggled the handle a bit, or it didn't actually jiggle, but—"

Tom smiled.

"Never even occurred to me."

They looked at each other. Tom was running his tongue alongside the inside of his lips, nodding deeply.

"Well," said Greg. "Let's give it a shot."

"I'll warn you now," said the woman. "You aren't going to break that glass."

Greg believed her, but he knew he would not be able to rest until he tried for himself. Tom unpacked his toolbox and Greg gave it one firm swing with the hammer, and the shockwave jolted back up his arm with a ringing firmness, as if he had just struck against solid steel. Tom was older than Greg and much shorter, but he insisted on taking a turn as well. They couldn't get a crowbar into the frame, and Tom's power drill had no effect on the lock, either. Greg sighed.

"Let's see what Google has to say," he said.

"No," said Tom, pulling out his cellphone. "Just one minute."

He dialed three numbers and Greg heard the phone ring six times before he finally got an answer.

"Right," said Tom, holding the phone to his ear as he lounged against his washing machine. "You don't say? Alright, alright. Well, let me ask you this: have any business owners called in about it? Or the reverse? Hmm… Well, thanks a lot."

Tom hung up the phone and looked at Greg.

"Apparently they've been taking calls about these things all morning, and it's not isolated to this area. According to the health department, they aren't radioactive or poisonous. So far no one has been injured, so they're not treating it as a threat. We're advised to change our locks, if we're concerned about employees sneaking through our homes, but otherwise they said we should be fine trying to ignore it. Curious thing: it's only happening to residences."

Greg nodded thoughtfully the entire time. He hadn't really expected to get any answers from the police department. Tom rubbed his chin, and then spoke again.

"So, where do we go from here? Sounds like it's gonna be a long time before we get any answers."

An idea occurred to Greg.

"You got a pair of binoculars? Maybe there's a phone number or something inside."

Tom smiled.

"Slipped my mind," he said. "But, yeah, the lady on the phone said they've got forensics examining one of the sites and they haven't found anything. Not so much as a scrap of actual English, beyond the front door. No clue who's doing it."

Greg thought about it, and then knelt down to squint inside again. He had assumed the words next to the pizzas were small, medium, and large, based on the pictures. But it was actually just a series of blurry smears. He stood back up and glanced at the window. It was already late afternoon, and he had work in the morning. Where could they go from here?

"I'll be next door. If I can think of anything, I'll let you know."

"Right," said Tom. "Same here."

A quick internet search showed countless new businesses showing up inside of apartments, all over the world. Apparently, they would not appear on any exterior wall, and they were always matched on opposite walls, so there was no opportunity to try tunneling in from the other side. The unscratchable firmness seemed to extend to all material these doors were connected to, so that even drywall was harder than diamond from any angle that would permit access. It was the same thing with all of them. Too small for practical use, no employees, always closed. People had tried shooting them, burning them, and cutting them, all to no avail. One YouTube video showed promise. A young man was using a laser pointer to conduct refraction experiments. But the beam behaved normally, passing through the front door of his miniature auto parts retailer and landing on the far wall without any visible distortion. Finally, the algorithm began to recycle itself, showing Greg the same articles and videos clips he had already seen.

Hours passed as Greg alternated between checking on the door and returning to the couch to refresh Google yet again. He was never going to relax with the convenience store inside his laundry room, and so far it had not disappeared. He checked every fifteen minutes. It was long past his usual bedtime when the internet finally turned over an interesting stone. CERN had called a press conference to announce that they were preparing to release a statement in a few hours.

Time slipped by like a turtle stranded in the desert, but there was no shortage of speculation from other corners of the internet about what the statement might entail. People discussed the Mandela Effect and alternate universes and posited that a parallel dimension might be attempting to make contact. Others pointed out that CERN routinely released statements, it's just that the news never really paid attention before. There were analyses of past press releases, attempting to discern whether CERN might have actually caused the phenomenon. Nothing to do but wait.

A sudden thought struck Greg as he sat scrolling in his living room. He still hadn't folded his laundry. He could kill fifteen minutes with that, easily. Plus, he had been trying to limit his inspections of the doorway, and this would give him an excuse to check in. He made his way through the kitchen, into the laundry room. The sign still said CLOSED. Nothing had changed inside. The door was still locked. He retrieved his clothes from the drier, noting that they were wrinkled.

He even made a point of closing his laptop before he went back to fetch the iron. With only the slightest effort of will, he refrained from checking on the door. It had only been a few seconds, anyway. Ironing would add another half hour. When that was finished, Greg made a pointed effort to avoid even checking the clock. He could throw on another chore, and bring CERN's statement even closer. The kitchen floor was not in particular need of sweeping, but he went through the motions anyway, depositing a meager pile of dust into the trash can.

Feeling even better, he considered going to sleep. It was nearly midnight. Down the hallway, the open door of his bedroom yearned invitingly. But he still needed to brush his teeth. It was as he was standing in front of the mirror, scrubbing away at his mouth, subconsciously avoiding the urge to check over his reflection's shoulder for new developments occurring inside his apartment, that the idea began to form. What if the door was just waiting for him to fall asleep? He spat the toothpaste from his mouth and rinsed and spat again but he could not dismiss the image of the door unlodging itself from the wall and sneaking down his hallway to smother him in his sleep.

It's just the lateness of the hour, he told himself. But he did not believe it. As he lay in bed drifting on the edge of sleep, he was haunted by transliminal images of waking up in a house that was gradually shrinking while the mysterious door enlarged as he stood on helplessly before it, trying to squeeze himself through the decreasing laundry room entrance, feeling his ribs crack and pop as his ceiling slowly cut off the light in front of him. And then it reversed, with the laundry room and door both growing to enormous proportions as he staggered and stuttered. The impulse to flee struck him far too late. His pace was sluggish, but it wouldn't have mattered, because the house was doubling in size every minute. It was soon impossible to even gain his bearings, as the washer and drier both began to simultaneously grow in size and recede in clarity, eventually sliding away into a wall of white fog beyond the horizon.

When he was suddenly jolted awake, it was just barely after midnight. He was disappointed by the sensation that it had all been a dream. There was no convenience store, no neighbor named Tom, no great mystery to solve. But then another idea struck him. He had first found the door immediately after midnight. Maybe it operated on some kind of daily schedule? Plus, there was still the CERN announcement to look forward to.

He wandered down the hall, pausing to grab a coke from the fridge. He drank it quickly, and the cold soda began to restore his focus as it pooled in his gut. He wanted to be alert if something new had happened. He stopped again, just outside the laundry room door, listening. If the theories about interdimensional portals were accurate, it was possible that the convenience store operated on an opposite timeline. Maybe their eight in the morning was our eight at night. Or perhaps the customers and employees had shut down their businesses due to general bewilderment about the sudden appearance of laundry rooms in their storage areas.

He debated between looking at the door itself and checking the news from CERN. And then he froze again. Perhaps it would be better to find some other way to occupy his time. It was not fear of danger that compelled him to wait, but rather fear of disappointment. There were three possible outcomes: the door was gone, the door had changed, or it had never existed. Judging by previous experience, the middle option was the least likely. He had lived his entire life in a world where either no strange doors existed in his laundry room or a singular unchanging door was firmly lodged in his laundry room. Never before had he encountered a scenario wherein the door was unlocked or the store occupied. Statistically speaking, he had to prepare himself for disappointment.

His kitchen was dark and empty, lit up by nothing more than the light of the oven clock. It occurred to him that he was already disappointed. He had been disappointed for a long time before the mysterious door showed up. Change was a constant factor of reality, but the changes tended to repeat themselves, slowly bringing things back towards a baseline of boredom. And Greg had to admit that the convenience store anomaly was actually far more fascinating as a hypothetical than a potential.

For the first time, he considered that the store might be a boon. Taking a seat on the couch, looking at the shadows cast on the wall by the dim yellow street lamps outside his curtains, he considered how the door might be able to benefit him, beyond serving as an object of curiosity. He'd already had a day off work. Undoubtedly he could take another. But how long could he live without money? The thought of money took him back to the store. Was there some way he might be able to conduct a transaction?

His first instinct was to press some cash up to the window. Doubtless the store was still empty of employees, but maybe there was a surveillance camera that might spot it. The thought of that intrigued him. It might have just been his mind playing tricks on him, but he could have sworn there was a faint reddish glow coming from behind the cash register the last time he had checked. Wait, he thought to himself. Although not open, the store might still be receiving power. Did it come from his apartment? Wouldn't hurt to check the breaker panel.

It was located in the laundry room, but his hesitation to check the door had evaporated, now that he had other options to extend his amusement. If there was nothing to do with the breaker panel, then he might have some luck connecting to the inside through bluetooth or wifi. He entered the room and gave the door a cursory glance. Still the same size, still CLOSED. The breaker panel was behind the washer, and he had to lean over to reach it. After he had pulled the latch and opened the small gray door, he suddenly remembered that he didn't really know what he was looking for. But luck was finally on his side, and it presented itself automatically.

Taped to the inside of the door, scrawled in some forgotten tradesman's looping handwriting, was a map of the breakers:

MAIN
LIVING ROOM/BATHROOM
KITCHEN/LAUNDRY
BEDROOM

Right now the KITCHEN/LAUNDRY switch was set to ON. Of course, in a parallel dimension, that must mean that the breaker was set to OFF. For a moment, he considered grabbing his phone and recording his impending discovery. And then he forced himself to calm down. Probably, nothing would happen. Just another of the long line of questions provoked by this bizarre anomaly, all of them answered with either 'I don't know' or 'no.' He considered taking a moment to distract himself from the question. Going for his camera was just the beginning. Why not boot up the laptop and see if anyone else had thought of it first? While he was dragging it out, he may as well go ask Tom if he'd given it a shot.

He was being dumb. If it were really going to be this simple, the scientists would have figured it out already. It was time to put this idiotic hope to rest.

Satisfied in his impending disappointment, Greg reached for the KITCHEN/LAUNDRY switch and was interrupted by a knock at the door. He didn't want to drag it out any further, but at the same time it didn't seem right that the moment of truth should be rushed. He tried to ignore it, but then there was a slightly louder knock. Greg leaned back and looked through the open laundry room door, past the kitchen. His lights were off, and he could see three shadows silhouetted against the yellow street lamp glow of the front window, on the other side of his curtains.

Who could that possibly be? What could they possibly want?

He heard Tom speak up.

"Was in here earlier. We spoke, and went down to the manager's office."

An unfamiliar voice responded.

"Well, does he know about it?"

There was a series of general statements.

"If he did, he'd be awake right now."

"Should we try the door?"

"We can't wait for him to figure it out on his own. It's just common decency."

Greg stepped gently through the living room, careful not to make a sound. He listened at the door, waiting to see if they would reveal the topic of discussion. He tried to create a psychic link, screaming in his mind that if they were truly worried about his safety, they might try shouting before forcing the door. He weighed the pros and cons to opening the door. It was obvious there was some kind of urgency about the mysterious epidemic of businesses. It must not be immediately harmful. They said he'd be awake, not outside. But still, curiosity compelled him.

He reached forward and twisted the handle. It hadn't even been locked. Opening the door, he found three men waiting for him. Tom, and two strangers, most likely neighbors Greg hadn't seen before. Tom smiled and took the initiative.

"See," he said, looking at the other two. "Told you he'd be awake."

Greg smiled.

"Busted," he said. "So what's the big deal?"

One of the other guys spoke up.

"Alright, there hasn't been a full breach anywhere yet, but CERN released a spectrographic analysis on the interior of a clothing store inside of someone's closet. Apparently these things are loaded with some kind of never-before-seen gas. No telling how it would react with our atmosphere."

When the man paused, Greg considered this information. It did not change his plan to test the breaker panel. Sensing his growing impatience, the man continued.

"And apparently, it's not even glass that the windows are made of, it's some kind of new polymer. Truly alien stuff, they say."

Greg did not react to this news, either. Now he was just waiting for the men to leave. For some reason, he instinctively rejected the idea of telling them about his plan to flip the breaker. They'd want to hang around afterwards and speculate. Now it seemed even more idiotic. No doubt the scientists had tried cutting power to one of these things already. But he could tell by Tom's face that he was excited at the prospect of contemplating this new information.

"Well," said Greg. "It sounds like they're getting it sorted out. What does it mean for us, though?"

Tom shook his head.

"I don't know, but I dislike the idea of being around one, right now. Figured you might not either. We're talking about new types of gasses, new types of materials. Who knows what kind of undetectable radiation they might be giving off?"

Greg let him continue. Tom talked for so long that he expected to see the glow of the sun over the horizon at every instant. He yawned and turned to check the time obnoxiously, the oven read one-fifteen, and Tom finally laughed and began winding down.

"I guess I'll let you get some rest. Just hope you wake up again tomorrow morning."

It was time to check the breaker. Greg liked to think of himself as a rational man, but he also had fun considering various superstitions. He took a moment to consider what a person who was suffering from delusions of reference might make of this situation. To such a person, nothing was without significance. The entire universe was either a reflection of, or a suggestion to, their subconscious. They would believe that the convenience store had materialized to make a statement about either convenience stores or laundry rooms. The solution, therefore, would not be found by uncovering more information about the convenience store, but rather in answering the universe's challenge with one of his own.

But it could be further broken down by considering that the universe, or his own subconscious, had directed him specifically to the breaker. Flipping the breaker would either do nothing or it would—

Without a moment of further delay, Greg marched into his laundry room and flipped the breaker. It did not provide him with the sense of satisfaction which he had been hoping for, because he still had to turn around in order to observe any change which might have taken place. He did it without ceremony or consideration.

The convenience store was now fully alight. The interior lamps threw a strip of pale fluorescent glow onto the floor of his darkened laundry room. He could now see the merchandise, and if he peered harder, another door behind the counter. He tried the handle, but the store was still CLOSED.

Now what? Post it to the internet? Go tell Tom about it? Sit still and wait for another bolt of inspiration?

He went back to delusions of reference. What if it were not himself which had gone crazy, but reality? The only way to be certain would be to challenge the universe's absurd belief that mysterious laundry room businesses could or should exist. How could he answer this challenge with one of his own? It needed to be sharp and sudden, like how you would prick a person's toe to see if they were faking unconsciousness.

The store represented commerce, and now there was light, which is what had triggered this epiphany. Greg needed to find the opposite of commerce, brought to him by the light. Religion. Was he religious? He could have easily chosen a dozen different sects into which to throw his newfound desire for faith, but instead he reverted back to a childhood memory. His parents had never taken him to church, but they had talked about going with their parents. Baptist. He was a baptist.

Where was the dividing line?

Commerce was unnatural, but beneficial. Religion was natural but, according to current mainstream opinion, harmful. He began to inventory his life, putting things into natural and unnatural categories. Soda: harmful? Unnatural? Obviously, he could never return to his job again. His apartment was also the result of commerce, and therefore unnatural. He would have to leave. The store could have it. His car would be staying behind, and he didn't care enough to wonder if the few possessions he owned, the ones which held any sentimental value, could qualify as natural. In fact, he was beginning to realize that with a bit of mental effort, he could make anything and everything seem 'natural.'

The human mind was funny like that. It suddenly occurred to him that human consciousness might be considered unnatural. It was time to stop thinking. His impulse was to leave. And so he went out the front door, into the chill of the early morning, and began walking. The impulse to run struck him, and it was not until he began to sweat that he realized how unnatural his clothing was. Daylight found him nude, jogging on the grass beside a road which led out of town. His genitals bounced uncomfortably from thigh to thigh, but that was the natural way. Greg had fixated on baptism as the key which had set him free, and so as he jogged, he periodically yelled out 'I'm baptist!' but as his breath had begun to falter, it had been reduced to just 'Baptist!'

Others had joined him, no doubt by now exhausted from trying to solve the mystery of the phantom businesses, and simply relieved that Greg had found some passable distraction. They were also shouting 'baptist' as frequently as their lungs would allow, although Greg doubted they understood why. And soon enough, as he had fallen into a walking spat and was now looking for a place to rest, someone else had joined the nude jogging pack. He was about Greg's age, and just as nude, but since he had only just joined, he seemed fresh and young and full of life.

The new man jogged up next to the crowd and then fell into stop alongside Greg, who had just regained enough breath to shout 'baptist' again, and looked him dead in the eye.

"Lutheran," spat the man, angrily. Greg stopped walking. The crowd stopped alongside him. Greg did not know the differences between Lutheranism and Baptism, and in fact he would have guessed that they were defined more by their similarities. It wasn't anything the young man said so much as his tone which had upset Greg and brought him to a halt. They'd had a good thing going here, and then this stranger had made a pointed effort to ruin it. No doubt a good Lutheran believed in keeping the peace, and yet this stranger had asserted his Lutheranism for no other visible purpose than to upset everyone else for the purpose of attention. He was sacrificing the sacred tenets of Lutheranism for his own personal advancement. Hypocrisy! And yet, whispers were spreading through the crowd:

"Lutheran?"

"Lutheran."

"Lutheran!"

Any moment now they would all be saying it and for all anyone could tell, Lutheranism was nothing more than a concerted attempt to enrage Baptists. The impulsive Baptist jogging pack was about to descend into calculated Lutheran chaos. The crowd was eyeing Greg. There was no precedent for challenges. And so, seized by a sudden impulse and aware that his efforts could never meet success, Greg simply shrugged and said:

"Lutheran."

Nightshift

By Ogden Nesmer

I used to perk up every time I'd hear the little bell over the door ring. I'd stand at attention and watch the bored, fat people perusing our selection. They'd lay their finds out in front of me and ask "box of Marlboros?" and at first it was kind of magical. The shelves were stocked during the day shift, and the cleaning crew only ever showed up sporadically. I had free-time and privacy. A place to think, or to not think. To doodle and read and get high. Free from work and stress, future prospects and life experience.

The little bell rang.

I've been here now longer than most of my supervisors. Always pimpled teens eager for any authority they can find, pointing up at me and telling me how to do my meaningless duty. They come and they go. I've seen it all; there is nothing to see. In all senses not legally binding this domain is mine. The only things that predate me and will exist long past my departure are the little plastic parcels of junk food. Sugar and salt. Soda and chocolate and cheese-dusted loops. I am their guardian. I belong to them.

"Pack of Newports?"

I grabbed the smokes without turning. I know exactly where they are on the tall rack behind me. I slid them through the portal in the fiberglass partition.

"Thanks," she said on the way out, and the little bell rang.

At night it's foggy and cold. Past the parking lot everything is shrouded. Nothing can be seen except for the occasional pair of headlights. They rush by like ghosts, driven, until one stops and turns its gaze at you.

I was running hot water over my fingers in the sink one winter night when I heard a sudden, metallic whine coming from the basement and the water turned cold. With one of the keys I'd been given on my first shift, but never actually used, I went down to investigate. There was an ancient water heater in the far corner of the unlit room. Something more akin to a boiler, it was gaunt and the black cast-iron panels met each other awkwardly from what I could see. It was releasing tiny burps of steam. I couldn't tell if this was by design. I touched it half-expecting to scald my hands but it was enticingly warm, and I stayed there touching it for several minutes.

My managers don't know about the basement. When I told the pimple-faced-teen of the time about the decrepit heater he advised me not to go down unless absolutely necessary. I was not covered for injuries sustained by heavy equipment that I was not authorized to use, he told me.

The bell rang, letting in a group of teenagers all laughing and joking loudly.

Teenagers are the worst customers. They steal more often than they buy. They are loud and unafraid to mock me openly, knowing I can do nothing. The bigger ones often try to intimidate me into selling them cigarettes and alcohol, then kick over trash cans when I refuse.

The group of them came to my counter and set a few bags of candy down, not looking at me. Not interested. I rang them up and they left, fading away into the fog, still laughing at some stupid joke.

I once had a manager who was not a pimpled teen. He was a harsh Iranian man of about fifty who spoke little English, and only ever in an impatient voice. He spent his first week giving the premises a close inspection, counting and cleaning everything in the building. He wanted to be let into the basement.

With a flashlight we could see it all clearly. The entire room was damp and humid. Dark spots clustered on the ceiling. The rafters and other wood surfaces were speckled with greasy mushrooms, and there was a rusty puddle stretching out from the base of the water heater. The manager pulled me out, suddenly disgusted and covering his mouth and nose. He put a second lock on the door and pocketed the key. He told me something would have to be done about this. He took the initiative in solving the problem. He was promoted, and he was soon gone. He took the key with him.

Just as the managers change, the customers are not regulars. They come from the city or they're passing through, but I do not recognize them. I doubt they recognize me.

"Wake up," he had said rapping his knuckles hard on the glass. He had friends with him, laughing. He wanted cigarettes but he couldn't have them so he got angry and started crashing into shelves and his friends were laughing and he started stomping on the snacks. Popping them like little firecrackers and launching crumbs all over the floor. I had to stop him; it comes out of my paycheck. I tried to say sir, because even though he was obviously just some kid he was towering huge, stomping around like a giant while his friends were laughing. Sir, I said, trembling until I started to say boy and he noticed me and started to throw his weight at the fiberglass.

"What did you say?" he demanded. "What did you just fucking say to me?"

His friends were laughing and the fiberglass wobbled making that fake thunder sound until it finally burst. They were laughing as he stepped over me and put his hands on the rack behind me and started pulling. He tore it down and heavy bottles of liquor fell onto me and shattered and cut me and spilled into my wounds.

My manager then told me I wasn't covered for the kind of injuries I sustained. And anyways the security cameras weren't on, he had said.

We keep tools in a metal shed; a drill, some socket wrenches, for some reason a rake. A pair of chain cutters and a hacksaw. I flipped the sign to closed on the front door and made my way back into the basement. I took about thirty minutes. It was warm inside. I didn't need a light. I ran my hand along the moist wooden paneling as I made my way to the heater. There seemed to be a sound coming from inside, so I pressed my cheek against its hull and listened. I heard it gurgle and whine, the sound coming from deep deep inside, like somebody crying at the bottom of a well.

One of my managers was not pleased to hear about my assault. It frustrated him vicariously. I believe he also hated teenagers the way I did. He gave me a gun in secret, before he too eventually left this place. It still sits under the counter always near my hand. When my attacker returns, which he won't, I will pull my gun out and kill him. I have thought about the consequences of this and I don't care. It will never happen anyway.

Once in the basement I found something new. It couldn't be new, but it had to be. A little steel latch on the back wall, because it wasn't a wall it was a door. But it couldn't be opened. I pushed and the wood oozed saturation like a sponge, but it did not open. We had no key for it. We had thousands of keys stashed in drawers and cabinets but they did not belong to the door. I checked. I threw all my weight into the wall again and again and knocked down some mushrooms, which hit the ground with oily splats.

The little bell rang.

They walked in, laughing. I heard them but I was busy trying to open the new door and I tried not to listen to them. I wanted to find the hinges but there didn't seem to be any. I pawed around, feeling moisture and mold decorating every inch but no hinges. They noticed my absence. Ain't nobody here, I heard one say. I ran my fingers along the ground to try and find the crack under the door to pry it up but there was nothing. I heard them laughing again, vicious, stuffing things in their pockets. Things were being broken, they were laughing. I grabbed the chain cutters and started hacking away at the soft, mushy wood. It sprayed me with each stab. Black water thick with filth and bacteria. The water heater was whining and burping and the commotion upstairs wound down. Someone said hello? I had the sharp end burrowed deep, wedged between the latch and the wood to try and pop it off and I pushed my weight and felt the wood creak. A hollow pop echoed as if down a long long hallway. Reverberating off walls into silence. They were looking for me upstairs now, and when he stood in the doorway watching me hungrily curious I didn't need to turn to know it was him. He had returned for me, he recognized me, as I him, and when I turned the cutters to him he sprayed too, wet on my face, and opened up to silence and then suddenly I was freed.

title

By Luiz Lapin

The following text has been collected and translated from the inbox of Fernanda Santos.

#

From: Francisco Santos <fsantos1234@hotmail.com>
Date: Tuesday, February 15th, 2005 at 9:24 PM
To: Fernanda Santos <nandasabc3@gmail.com>
Subject: Re: oi

   Hey, Sis!
   I know haven't e-mailed you in a while, but it took some time to get internet installed. At least it's faster than it was back home. I can even watch videos without having to wait an hour for them to load! I actually got this computer for a really good price at a thrift store down the street. It's not the best, but it's still way better than my old one.

Anyway, the guy from the restaurant said I should come back for an interview next week. Looks like there are gonna be plenty of long hours, but being undocumented doesn't really give me a ton of options. I hope it works out. The money is running out and I don't want to get behind on rent.

My new landlord is surprisingly nice, but I want to keep it that way. I even asked Mr. Silva what the catch was, since this is the cheapest place in the neighborhood. He just laughed it off and said that most people are bothered by the idea of living in a place with no windows.

As long as there aren't any ghosts, I think I should be fine hahaha!

Anyway, it's good to hear that Manu is getting better! Please tell her that Uncle Frankie is going to send her a very special gift! You won't believe how cheap those Disney plushies are around here, and I have a feeling that I'll be able to send more money soon.

Did she actually believe those old wives' tales about the duendes? That's hilarious! I think it's great that you're sharing this stuff with Manu. I used to love mom's stories, even if we were too afraid to sleep after hearing them.

Speaking of duendes, there's something funny going on around here. I know it sounds silly, but a few of my socks have gone missing this past week. The basement isn't that big and there aren't many places that I could have lost them, so I'm really confused.

Don't worry, it's not a basement like the one in grandpa's old place. There's a separate entrance outside, and everything is divided into rooms - kind of like an underground apartment. I actually think it's kind of cozy. The house above is rented to a Korean family, but I haven't had the chance to introduce myself yet.

I really wish you and Manu were here with me, Nanda. It's a beautiful country, especially now in the wintertime, but it gets lonely after a while. I'm still not entirely used to the snow, but even I have to admit that it's a wonderful sight.

Love you! And tell Manu to watch out for mail in the future!

\#

From: Francisco Santos <fsantos1234@hotmail.com>
Date: Wednesday, February 23rd, 2005 at 7:31 PM
To: Fernanda Santos <nandasabc3@gmail.com>
Subject: Re: trampo

Hi, Sis!

You don't have to worry about money anymore! After a bit of training, they took me in at the restaurant. Now you can use the money you had saved up to go out with Manu. Take her to see that new robot movie or something, I know she'd love that.

To be honest, it's been a rough week, but I think things are finally going to be alright. Mr. Hasan is a cool boss, and I think it's hilarious that this "authentic Italian restaurant" is run by an old Middle Eastern man. The customers don't seem to mind, though. Most of the other workers aren't local either, which makes me feel more at home. That's a rare feeling these days.

I spend most of my time cleaning dishes and sweeping the floors (you'd be surprised with how much of a mess these *gringos* can make, especially in such a tiny little restaurant), but Mr. Hasan says he'll give me a spot as a waiter when my English gets better. He even trusts me enough to let me close up shop all by myself. It's still a lot of work for so little pay, but I'm grateful for it, and it's only a 15-minute subway ride away.

I also met this really nice Croatian girl that helps me to clean up after the place is closed. She always ties her hair up in a ponytail and has these really cute bangs. I'm considering asking her out. I'm not sure how we'll communicate since her English isn't very good either, but loneliness outweighs embarrassment at this point. Guess I need some company in my cold little hobbit hole, hahahaha.

Oh, and remember that missing sock mystery? I decided to try and take the dryer apart to see if I could find anything, but when

I dragged the machine away from the wall, I found something strange in the tile underneath.

There's a tiny hole on the floor, about the size of an Oreo. When I got close, I could feel air flowing into it. I was a little worried at first, thinking that there might be some sort of gas leak or rodent infestation, but I couldn't see anything in there even with a flashlight. I taped a piece of cardboard over it - just in case.

Weird, right? I hope there aren't any duendes living in there, hahaha!

By the way, how have you girls been holding up? I know we don't talk about it much, but I'm aware that things have been hard since grandma passed. Just remember that I'm still your big bro, even on the other side of the world. I'm going to try and get one of those international phone cards so we can catch up properly later this week.

In the meantime, I finally sent you girls that present! They said that it might take a while to get there, but I just hope that they don't confiscate it like that time Andressa tried to send us those videogames.

Love you, and I'll keep you updated!

PS: I wasn't sure whether to mention this or not, but I just can't get it out of my head. I was curious about how deep the hole was, so I threw a penny inside and waited to hear it clang against something. It didn't make a sound. It's probably nothing, but you never know…

#

From: Francisco Santos <fsantos1234@hotmail.com>
Date: Saturday, March 5th, 2005 at 10:53 PM
To: Fernanda Santos <nandasabc3@gmail.com>
Subject: buracos

Hey Sis!

First of all, I really enjoyed our talk over the phone. It felt great to speak in our own language for a while. I hope you enjoyed hearing about my first date in this country! I'm still not sure what to make of it, but I think I'll be seeing Mia again soon.

It's hard for us to understand each other sometimes, but our little after-hours conversations are one of the only things keeping me sane at this point. I don't think she knows just how much she's been helping me.

However... that's not why I'm e-mailing you.

Some more stuff started to go missing around the basement. At first, I thought I was just misplacing things. Small stuff, like pens and toothbrushes. But last night I freaked out when I got home from work and found my fridge door open. It was completely empty!

My first thought was that someone had broken in, but that didn't make any sense. Why would a thief just raid the fridge and leave everything else behind? But it gets weirder. That night, I dreamt about the little hole I found underneath the dryer. It had been in the back of my mind for a while now, and in the dream I heard a voice calling me from inside. It sounded like *me*. When I woke up, I decided to pull back the dryer and check on it again. Just in case.

The piece of cardboard I had left there was gone, and there were more holes this time. I counted five of them spread across the floor. The biggest one is about the size of a fist, and the air flow is a lot stronger now.

But that's not all. I know this sounds insane, but the holes are lined with a single row of jagged little teeth, like a leech or something. I cut my finger on one of them while I was trying to get a closer look, and I swear I saw it *move*. It makes no sense, Sis.

When I shine the flashlight inside them it's like the dark just goes on forever. I can't explain it. Maybe it's some kind of freaky mold?

I'm a little scared but I don't know who else to talk to about this. I don't think it's smart to draw attention to myself right now, and I don't want people to think I'm crazy either, but I can't just ignore it. I'll try talking to Mr. Silva. Maybe he'll know what to do.

One more thing. I got an e-mail from the postal service while

I was writing this. They said that the package I sent you is going to be late due to content inspection =/

Anyway, love you girls to death, and I hope we can talk again soon.

#

From: Francisco Santos <fsantos1234@hotmail.com>
Date: Saturday, March 12th, 2005 at 11:59 PM
To: Fernanda Santos <nandasabc3@gmail.com>
Subject: Re: vc tá tomando seus remédios?

I'm not crazy, Sis. I swear I'm not.

I don't want to scare you but something happened today and I don't know who else I can turn to.

The landlord finally came around this afternoon. I told him it was urgent but didn't give him any details over the phone. I practically dragged him into the laundry room when he arrived. He's a big Portuguese man, and kind of looks like Uncle Sandro with his little round glasses.

By the time he got here, the mouths had already spread to one of the walls. They're getting bigger, too. You could fit a soccer ball through the larger ones.

Mr. Silva thought it was a prank at first, but he stopped smiling when I extended the measuring tape into one of the mouths on the floor. Five meters, and still no end in sight. Same thing with the ones on the wall. It made no sense.

After that, he was just as scared as I was. I actually had to convince him not to call the cops. Besides, even if they believed him, it's not like they would know more than we did. I told him about the missing stuff and how it appeared to be getting worse, so he suggested that we try to remove one of the mouths ourselves.

Mr. Silva tried using a paint scraper at first, but we soon realized that the mouths had no edge to scrape. He ended up slipping and losing the tool inside one of them. Then, he went to his truck and came back with a hammer and a chisel. After making a bit of a mess, I helped him to remove a hand-sized piece of tile from the floor, with one of the mouths still attached. We were expecting to see the rest of some ungodly creature dangling from the other side, but we didn't find anything beneath the tile. The mouth, and the void inside it, is somehow only on the surface.

We sat in silence for a while, thinking about what we saw. Then, we began to talk about what these things could be. The mouths were clearly alive and "eating" things, but we had no way of knowing if they were somehow attached to something else or how far they could spread.

At one point, Mr. Silva also suggested that it could be some kind of mold. Deep down, we both knew it couldn't be anything that simple, but we were trying to rationalize the situation and figured that we could try to get rid of the thing with heat or fungicide.

Mr. Silva took out a cheap lighter from his pocket and lit it up next to one of the smaller mouths on the wall. Its teeth began to quiver and the thing *hissed* at us in response, as if it were in pain.

We were startled for a bit, then Mr. Silva handed me the keys to his truck and told me to bring back the red gallon of gas that he keeps in the back. I was only gone for about a minute or so, but that was enough for things to go wrong.

When I came back into the laundry room, I found him lying on his side, still holding onto the lighter. His head was fucking gone, Nanda. I don't mean bitten or cut off, just gone, as if he never had one to begin with. There was no blood. Smooth skin covered his neck where a wound should have been.

I rushed to his side, but there was nothing to be done. I don't know if he tried to look inside one of the mouths or if they sensed that we were trying to get rid of them and attacked him, but it was too late. He still had a pulse, though. I don't know how, but his heart was still beating.

I sat there for ages, thinking about who to call and who might believe me. I can't risk getting deported, Sis. Not after all we've been through. Not when I'm so close to making things work.

I think I know what to do now. I can make Mr. Silva disappear. Then I'll take his truck back to his house. His wife died a few years ago and he doesn't have any kids, so no one will show up to ask questions. At least not right away. I know it's not fair to him, but I don't have a choice.

When I've saved up some money, I'll be able to leave this place. Then I'll do the right thing and tell someone about what happened. I promise.

I miss you and Manu so much, Nanda.

#

From: Francisco Santos <fsantos1234@hotmail.com>
Date: Wednesday, March 30th, 2005 at 7:30 AM
To: Fernanda Santos <nandasabc3@gmail.com>
Subject: Re: volte pra casa!!!

Hey, Nanda. I'm sorry I haven't returned your calls. I needed some time to process everything that happened. But I'm okay now. You don't have to worry about me.

I did what I had to do. What happened to Mr. Silva wasn't my fault and beating myself up about it isn't going to help anyone. I'd rather not discuss the details regarding the "incident" and how I dealt with it, but I think I finally got my life back on track.

I had to miss a few days at work in order to clean things up, but Mia covered for me and Mr. Hasan is convinced that I just had the flu. I won't lie to you, Sis. Those first few days were rough. I felt sick all the time and just wanted to end things once and for all. But I kept thinking of you and Manu. To give up now would be selfish.

I dreamt a lot during that time. At first, about Mr. Silva. I kept reliving what I did to him and it was like torture. But then, something strange happened… I started to forget. All my memories about Mr. Silva are fading. I don't even remember how I found out about this basement, and even his name feels *wrong* when I type it. Maybe it's for the best.

Eventually, I started dreaming about the mouths again. They spoke to me, repeating the same word again and again. "Flesh". I can't explain it, but I know these aren't just dreams. They're messages.

After a while, I realized that the mouths had stopped spreading and nothing else had gone missing since I fed Mr. Silva to them. That's when I realized what I had to do to keep things under control.

I buy meat at the supermarket now. Usually chicken feet and heads, but sometimes a bit of ground beef too. Whatever is cheapest. I feed the mouths once a day, just a little bit at a time. They've mostly left me alone since I started. Feeding them is kind of expensive but it's better than the alternative. I still haven't been sleeping right, though.

When I finally went back to work, Mia knew that something was wrong immediately. She said I looked sick and asked if I'd been eating properly. I told her I was dealing with some personal issues and left it at that. I don't want to drag her into this mess, but she's been helping me out so much. I've actually been spending a lot of time at her place. She wants to visit the basement, but I keep making excuses, telling her that something's wrong with the plumbing and that the Landlord doesn't like it when I have guests over. So far, she doesn't seem to mind. The days are getting warmer, so we spend a lot of time outdoors anyway. I wish you could meet her, Sis.

I'm glad that things are finally going back to "normal". If I can call it that. I've been keeping the laundry room door closed and doing my laundry at a coin-operated place across the street. On a good day, I forget that the mouths are even there.

If I can keep this up, I should be able to save enough money to move somewhere else soon.

Love you very much, Sis. Never forget that.

I'll call you soon. =)

#

From: Francisco Santos <fsantos1234@hotmail.com>
Date: Friday, April 15th, 2005 at 7:22 AM
To: Fernanda Santos <nandasabc3@gmail.com>
Subject: Re: vc precisa de ajuda

Hey, Sis.

Remember how Grandma used to say that everything happens for a reason, but sometimes we have to make that reason ourselves? I think I finally understand what she meant.

Things were fine around here for a little while. I was managing to keep some sort of routine - feeding the mouths, going to work and hanging out with Mia. Sometimes, I could almost pretend I was living a normal life. Every now and again I would wake up in the middle of the night feeling like a piece of shit, but the feeling would go away when I remembered why I came here in the first place.

Then the dreams started up again. "Flesh", the mouths repeated in a nightly choir of my own voice. Sleep was impossible. I guess life always finds a way to remind us how little control we have over things.

At first, I thought if I kept things the way they were, the mouths would eventually stop bothering me. Then one day, I woke up on the floor. My bed was missing. When I opened the laundry room to check on the mouths, I nearly lost my foot in one of them. They had taken over the entire room. Walls, floor, ceiling - the entire thing was like a freakish honeycomb of hungry mouths of varying sizes. Some of the older ones were so big that you could practically fall into them.

After that, I tried to buy more meat, but I just couldn't keep up. They always wanted more, and I was already having trouble feeding myself, not to mention saving up money to leave this godforsaken place. Eventually, they ate my TV. Then they went after some of my shoes.

That's when I started to take stuff from the restaurant. It was just table scraps at first. I would wait until everyone else had left and collect pieces of leftover meat from the dirty dishes and trash cans.

Someone must have noticed, as Mr. Hasan eventually found out and came to talk to me. I told him the scraps were for my dog, but he knew something was up. He had caught me sleeping on the job a couple of times and thought that I was looking under the weather. He said I could tell him if something was wrong and claimed that he just wanted to help. I wanted to tell him the truth but I didn't know how, so I just promised him that it wouldn't happen again. He let me off with a warning.

The scraps helped for a little while, but the dreams came back after about a week. I wasn't about to wait for the damned things to take over the rest of the basement, so I did the only thing I could do. I started raiding the restaurant's walk-in freezer. I'd always wait until Mia had left, though. I couldn't bear the thought of her thinking I was a thief.

I looked for expired cans and stuff that I didn't think was going to be missed, but that only kept the mouths satisfied for a few days. When I realized that wasn't enough, I started taking large chunks of frozen meat.

I felt awful stealing from Mr. Hasan, but I had no choice. Besides, it was only temporary. I just needed to keep things under control until I had enough money to move out.

Then, last night Mr. Hasan forgot his keys and came back inside the restaurant while I was in the freezer. He found me with a bag full of frozen chickens. I didn't know how to explain myself without sounding like a crazy person, so I just begged him not to call the cops. I couldn't risk getting deported, not after everything I had been through. He felt sorry for me and didn't call anyone, but I was obviously fired.

I called Mia when I got home. I didn't mention the specifics, but I explained that I was worried about the basement now that I lost my job and didn't know what to do.

I think she knew I wasn't telling her the full story, but we ended up going out for late night hot dogs. After we ate, we walked around downtown talking about things we missed from our "old countries". She talked about something called *scampi* and I mentioned Grandma's old tapioca cake recipe. Then I told her about my plan to bring you and Manu to live here, and how I was worried about the future.

That's when Mia said something incredible. She asked me if I wanted to move in with her. After a moment of stunned silence, I answered her with a kiss.

To make a long story short, Mia is coming over tomorrow with her neighbor's car to help me move out. I can hardly wait.

I know I should be worried about money, but maybe getting fired was a blessing in disguise. I can find a new job, and the further away I get from this basement the better.

I just need to hold on for a little longer and everything will be fine. I know it will.

Love you, Nanda. Tell Manu I said "hi".

#

From: Francisco Santos <fsantos1234@hotmail.com>
Date: Saturday, April 16th, 2005 at 5:45 PM
To: Fernanda Santos <nandasabc3@gmail.com>
Subject: Re: me responda

I messed up, Sis.

All I can do now is tell you what happened, even though I know you're not going to believe me.

Mia came by this afternoon like we had agreed. Seeing her face was like looking at the sun after waking up from a nightmare. I gave her a tour of the place, but there wasn't much to see. The mouths had already taken most of what I owned.

I made an effort not to leave her alone once we started packing, and I kept the laundry room door shut the entire time. "Black mold," I told her.

She was obviously weirded out by how empty the place was, especially when she saw that my bed was missing. I explained that I had gotten rid of some stuff to make the move easier. I don't know if she believed me. Honestly, I barely remember even owning a bed.

Along the way I showed her that picture of me and you from our trip to Rio. I told her about how you nearly pissed your pants at the top of that rickety old Ferris wheel next to the shopping mall. She said she'd love to meet you some day, and I promised that I'd tell her all the other embarrassing stories once the move was over.

It didn't take very long to box things up. I don't have that many clothes and I couldn't care less about the few pieces furniture that the mouths hadn't eaten. After about an hour or so, all the boxes were in the car. Looking back on it, I wish I had just left everything behind and ran while we still could.

We were carrying the last few boxes outside when the laundry room door started to rumble, as if someone was trying to force it open from the inside. Startled, Mia dropped the box she was carrying and blurted out a series of what I can only imagine were Croatian expletives. When the noise ceased, she started asking questions. I explained that it was just the plumbing acting up, but she wasn't convinced. The stubborn girl wanted to look inside.

I reminded her about the mold.

She said it would just be a quick peek.

Heart firmly lodged in my throat, I said no.

She just stood there for a moment, looking me over as I tried to come up with a more convincing excuse. For the first time since I met her, I think she was *afraid*. Before I could say anything, there was an awful gurgling sound, and the laundry room began to bleed.

The red reached her shoes and Mia gave me a nervous glance before rushing over to the door. I tried to grab her but it was already too late. Before she could even touch it, the entire door was ripped off its hinges by a gust of unnatural wind. The mouths ate the door. Then they ate Mia.

I screamed until I lost my voice, smashing furniture into the mouths and demanding that they take me instead. They didn't answer. I don't think they're ever going to stop.

It's so cold in here now. It's like they're eating the warmth.

I don't know what to do now, Nanda. Mia was all I had. This is all my fault and I don't know how to fix it. I should never have come here.

#

From: Francisco Santos <fsantos1234@hotmail.com>
Date: Sunday, April 17th, 2005 at 4:03 PM
To: Fernanda Santos <nandasabc3@gmail.com>
Subject: mia

i crid until i passed ot on the couch last niht.

then i begn to dream again.

i was in te basment surrounded by mouts in every direction. i askd what they wanted bt they didn't anser. i wantd to know where thy tok mia so i lookd inside one of thm. in th abyss i caught a glimps of their ful form. i wish i hadnt. from th insid out, they lok like suckrs on infinite limbs sukng debris ito a gaping void in the centr. i had it al wrong, nanda. its just prspctive. the mouths arnt growng, thyr getting closr. and when th thing gets her it wil eat an eat and et,util thres nothing left. we r jus here to feed the horribl things tht float n the dark.

i woke up screming an saw that more mouths ha startd snaking out of the laundry rom in a starshaped pattrn, searchng for mor food around the basment. this is ther home now, thy dont ned me anymore.

then i noticd my rigt hand was gone. the mouts must have gotten t it while i slep. the stump is somehw closd off with skin but i can stil feel everyting. its digesting me on the othr side ad god it hurts so fuckng bad.

but if i cn feel this then maybe mia is stll in there and hurting too. i hav to get hr back. im startng to forget hr face. i cant let that happn. i stll hav gasolin so ill tell it to giv her back to me or ill burn evrythng to the grnd.

i wont let it hrt anyone else.

i love yu and manu so mch nanda, im so sorry.
please pray fr me.

#

From: Andressa Santos <dessas4nt0s@gmail.com>
Date: Wednesday, April 20th, 2005 at 10:14 AM
To: Fernanda Santos <nandasabc3@gmail.com>
Subject: VEJA ISSO PRIMA

Hi, Nanda!
I thought you should see this:
TWO BODIES FOUND AFTER MYSTERIOUS BLAZE
Residents of the uptown area were caught by surprise late last night when a fire began raging in a two-story home. Firefighters arrived quickly at the scene and managed to control the blaze while also evacuating a family of three from the main floors. Unfortunately, the charred remains of a man and a woman were found in the basement, which appeared to be the source of the inferno. Authorities claim that basement was completely empty save for the two bodies, which were found huddled over an empty gallon of gas. This has led to speculation that the fire may have been intentional. There's still no word on the identities of the victims (…) Copied from The Metropolitan Express – 18/04/2005
Do you think it could be him???

#

From: Postmaster <postmaster@autoreply.com>
Date: Wednesday, April 20th, 2005 at 10:20 AM
To: Fernanda Santos <nandasabc3@gmail.com>
Subject: MESSAGE COULD NOT BE DELIVERED - Manu
<fsantos1234@hotmail.com> could not be found.

Undelivered Message:
Francisco, please answer my calls!
I'm so sorry!

Luiz Lapin

The package you sent finally arrived in the mail. I gave the box to Manuela and she took it to her room. A few minutes later, I heard a scream. I ran to Manu and found her crying in the corner. The package was open on her bed. I looked inside and I saw it, Francisco.

A   *mouth.*

Unreal Press is an independent small press publisher focusing on providing promising young writers the tools and platform to grow into the best writers of a generation. We target transgressive fiction and poetry for publishing.

If you enjoyed the stories in this anthology, subscribe to our newsletter to be notified of upcoming releases and free sneak peeks. You can also email unrealpressandpodcast@proton.me for inquires, feedback, review copies, and more.

Please leave an honest review on the Amazon store page.
We would like to hear about your experience!

Printed in Great Britain
by Amazon

27771983R00101